"Johnny talked about you from time to time, but I gather he said little about me."

"He mentioned R.T. a couple of times but no, he didn't say much. But then he didn't talk much about his friends in the Rangers or later. It was like when he came home, he turned all that off."

"Probably wise," Ryker said. He washed down a mouthful of bagel with some coffee. "Compartmentalizing, we call it. Keeping things separate. Why would he want to bring any of that home to you?"

"But he talked about me," she argued.

"Once in a while. Sometimes everyone talked about home. Sometimes we needed to remember that there was a place or a person we wanted to get back to. The rest of the time we couldn't afford the luxury."

That hit her hard, but she faced it head-on. Remembering home had been a luxury? That might have been the most important thing anyone had told her about what Johnny had faced and done.

"I didn't know him at all," she whispered, squeezing her eyes shut, once again feeling the shaft of pain.

"You knew the best part of him. That mattered to him, Marisa. You gave him a place where that part could flourish."

* * *

CONARD COUNTY: THE NEXT GENERATION

Dear Reader,

An event occurred shortly before I proposed this book: I faced the very difficult time a family goes through when they don't know what really happened to a loved one. It got me to thinking about how I'd feel if I were widowed and didn't believe the story I was told.

When it happens in your world, there are lots of things you can do to seek the truth. When it's a government agency providing the explanation of how your husband died overseas, it's harder to seek answers. And it's even harder when your husband's friend shows up months later and tells you the same story you don't believe.

Here we have the story of a pregnant widow who cannot believe she knows the truth, and of her late husband's friend, who seeks to help her and give her a more satisfying answer.

Sometimes the truth can never be revealed. But sometimes love can provide a balm.

Rachel Lee

An Unlikely Daddy

Rachel Lee

HARLEQUIN®SPECIAL EDITION®

Recycling programs
for this product may
not exist in your area.

ISBN-13: 978-0-373-65974-6

An Unlikely Daddy

Rachel Lee was hooked on writing by the age of twelve and practiced her craft as she moved from place to place all over the United States. This *New York Times* bestselling author now resides in Florida and has the joy of writing full-time.

Books by Rachel Lee

Harlequin Special Edition

Conard County: The Next Generation

The Lawman Lassoes a Family
A Conard County Baby
Reuniting with the Rancher
Thanksgiving Daddy
The Widow of Conard County

Montana Mavericks: 20 Years in the Saddle!

A Very Maverick Christmas

Harlequin Romantic Suspense

Conard County: The Next Generation

Guardian in Disguise
The Widow's Protector
Rancher's Deadly Risk
What She Saw
Rocky Mountain Lawman
Killer's Prey
Deadly Hunter
Snowstorm Confessions
Undercover Hunter
Playing with Fire
Conard County Witness
A Secret in Conard County

Visit the Author Profile page
at Harlequin.com for more titles.

To all the heroes whose stories will never be told.

Prologue

Marisa Hayes stood atop a hill in the Good Shepherd Cemetery in Conard County, Wyoming. The ceaseless spring wind seemed to blow through her hollow heart, sweeping away her life. Johnny's coffin, wood and brass, sat atop the bier, ready to be lowered. Beneath it a strip of artificial turf covered the gaping hole in the ground that would soon contain him. The green swatch was an affront to the brown ground all around.

She couldn't move. Pain so strong it was almost beyond feeling, a strange kind of agonized numbness, filled her. Several men were waiting to lower the casket. A few of her friends waited behind her, giving her space and time. Dimly she realized they must be growing impatient as time continued its inexorable march into a future she wished would go away.

Beyond the coffin she saw the tombstones of others

who had left this life before Johnny, generations of markers, some newer, some so old they tilted. Plastic flowers brought artificial color here and there to a comfortless landscape. No well-tended ground, this. No neatly trimmed lawns and shrubs trying to create an impression of life amidst death. Just the scrubby natural countryside, tamed to a level one could walk through, but no more. A couple of tumbleweeds had rolled in and hung up just since she arrived here. They'd move on soon. Everything moved on. Time stole everything, one way or another.

Her hand rested against her still-flat belly. She'd never had a chance to tell Johnny. If she believed the pastor, her husband knew. She wasn't sure if she believed the pastor. Right now she didn't know if she believed in afterlife, God or anything at all.

What she believed in was her pain. What she believed in was that she was carrying Johnny's baby. What she believed was that when she had tried to Skype him, to tell him, she had been told he was out, they'd give him a message. What she believed was that the next thing she heard was that Johnny was dead.

No open coffin. They'd warned against it. The funeral director had practically fallen on his knees, begging her not to demand it. Telling her that some images were best not remembered. Telling her to remember Johnny alive.

If the funeral director couldn't pretty it up...

But, no, she refused to go there. It was the one piece of advice she had taken. Holding the folded flag in her arms, against her baby, she could still hear the ring of "Taps" on the desolate air, could still feel the moment she had accepted that flag, as if it were the moment she had accepted Johnny's death. Then the man, someone she didn't know, a State Department official who had given his name, as if she cared, had said, "John was a true hero."

So? He was a dead hero, and his widow just wanted to climb into that hole beside him.

She lifted her gaze to the insensitive blue sky, wondering why it wasn't gray and weeping, the way her heart wept. Why thunder and lightning weren't rending the heavens the way her heart was rent.

She thought about burying the flag with Johnny. Just marching the four steps and placing it on the coffin. He'd earned that flag, not her, and right now it felt almost like an insult, not an honor. But she didn't do it. The baby. Someday the child within her might want this flag, all it would ever have of its father except a few photographs. Maybe someday it would even mean something to *her*.

"Marisa." Julie's quiet voice, near her. A touch on her arm. "We need to go."

"Then go."

"I think I was including you in that."

She turned her head, her neck feeling stiff, and looked straight into Julie's worried face. "I...can't."

"Yes, you can. Come on, hon. You can come back tomorrow if you want. You can come every single day. But right now..."

Right now people were waiting for her, waiting to take her home, waiting to put Johnny in the ground. When she came back tomorrow, the turf would still be there, covering the bare, freshly turned earth. But Johnny's coffin wouldn't be where she could see it. His final home.

Numbly she nodded, facing the inevitable. Everything seemed inevitable now. She felt like a leaf caught in a rushing river's grip, unable to stop anything, unable to catch her breath, unable find the shore. Adrift, banging from one rock to the next, helpless.

Despite Julie's entreaties, she walked up to the coffin and laid her hand on the cold, polished wood. "I love you," she whispered, hoping he could hear, fearing he couldn't.

Then, jerking with every single movement as if her body belonged to someone else, she allowed Julie to lead her back to her friends and the row of cars.

It was over. Tomorrow loomed like a devouring dragon. She hoped it devoured her.

Chapter One

Ryker Tremaine pulled up to the Hayes house on a frigid November night and looked at it from within the warm confines of his car. He needed to go in there, introduce himself to John's widow and start making amends. He suspected what John's death had cost Marisa, but it was only when word had sifted back to him that she was pregnant that he realized he had a whole hell of a lot of atoning to do. Because of him there was not only a widow, but a fatherless child.

He had some stains on his soul, but this one felt bigger than most, and some were pretty big.

It was a large house. He knew it had been in John's family for generations, because John had told him. It was, in John's mind, a safe place for Marisa to stay. She had grown up around here, too. She had a job at the community college, she had friends to look after her when her husband was away. And neither of them had any family left, odd as that seemed. Even Ryker, at almost forty, had parents who had retired to New Mexico and a sister who had married a sheep rancher from New Zealand. Somehow Marisa and John, through the vicissitudes of illness and life, had been left alone.

And now Marisa had no one but friends. Had she been blessed with a big family, he'd have felt his mission of repentance was pointless. But there was a woman and a baby who John Hayes couldn't look after. He owed something to John, to that woman and to that baby.

Just what, he wasn't sure. Conscience and a vague promise to John had driven him here, and now conscience kept him inside the car when he should have just strode up to the door and introduced himself.

She'd had nearly six months. Maybe someone out of her husband's past would only refresh her grief. And maybe he was making excuses because he dreaded this whole thing.

He wasn't a chicken by nature.

Sighing, he glanced in the rearview mirror, taking stock as much as he could. He'd ditched the suit because it was too much around here, and had settled on a sweater, jeans and a jacket. He didn't want this to look official, or remind her of bad things more than necessary.

But he continued to sit in the car a little while longer, wondering if this was just a huge act of selfishness on his part. He'd been wrestling with that since the thought of coming here had first begun goading him.

Penance was fine, as long as it didn't inflict pain on someone else. Atonement should make things better, not worse. He shouldn't salve his own guilt by worsening her pain.

He'd finally gotten to the point where he could no longer tell what was right or wrong, whether he was being selfish or paying a debt he owed a friend.

There was only one way to find out. That was to knock on the door and introduce himself. If she told him to go to hell, he'd have his answer. And maybe that wouldn't freshen her grief too much, just to hear someone say, "John was my friend."

Finally, he climbed out of the car, crunched his way across a sidewalk covered with rock salt and went up the porch steps. Icicles hung from the eaves, probably from a recent, brief thaw. If she didn't tell him to get out of her life immediately, he should knock them down. They weren't huge, but they could be dangerous, and she shouldn't do it herself in her condition.

At last he could avoid the moment no longer. The doorbell glowed, demanding he punch it and then face whatever came. Usually that wasn't a problem for him. Most things in his life had come at him the hard way. But this time…well, this time was different.

He rang the bell. He waited as the winter night deepened. She must be gone. Well, he'd come back tomorrow.

Then he heard the doorknob turn and the door opened. He recognized her instantly from photos John had shown him. Long ash-blond hair, eyes that were shaded somewhere between blue and lavender, set in a heart-shaped face. Her lips, soft and just full enough, framed the faintest of quizzical smiles. And her belly… He couldn't help but look at the mound. John's baby, due in a few months.

"May I help you?" Her voice was light, pleasant, but cautious.

He dragged his gaze to her face, understanding in an instant what had drawn John to her. Surprise shook him as attraction gut-punched him. He figured he must be plumbing new depths of ugliness. His friend's pregnant widow? Off-limits. He cleared his throat. "Hi," he said. "My name's Ryker Tremaine."

If he expected her to recognize it, he was disappointed. Her brow creased slightly. "Yes?" No recognition, nothing.

"I was John's friend," he announced baldly. "We worked together at…State. Before that, a few times when he was in the Rangers."

Her smile faded, but at least she didn't pale. "He never mentioned you."

He'd anticipated this possibility. The question was whether he should just walk away or press. He nodded. "He used to call me R.T."

"R.T.?" The furrow deepened, and then recognition dawned. "Oh. Oh! I thought he was saying Artie. Short for…" She clapped her hand to her mouth, as if containing something, and her face paled a little. "You were with him."

"Not that day," he said evenly. This wasn't going the way he'd imagined, good or bad. "I'm sorry. I'll leave you alone. I just…when I heard you were…" He glanced down.

Her hand dropped from her mouth to the mound of her belly. "Oh." She sounded faint and closed her eyes. Then they opened, blue fire. "Is there a reason for this visit after all this time?"

"I couldn't get away when…" He didn't want to say funeral. "Then I thought it was too late. And then I heard about… Maybe you have some questions I can answer."

At once he wanted to kick himself, because those were questions he mostly couldn't answer. He was usually better than this. Smoother. This was turning into a hash. "I've been out of the country," he finished finally. That was absolutely true.

She looked down. He braced for her to tell him to go to hell, a place he was intimately familiar with. But then, with a visible shake, she said, "Come in. I'm going to freeze standing here." She stepped back, allowing him to pass.

The house was warm and quiet except for the laboring forced air heat. A pleasantly sized foyer welcomed him, speaking of age and care. She pointed to his right. "Get yourself a seat in there. Do you want a hot drink?"

"I'm fine, Mrs. Hayes. If you want something, don't mind me. I'm not trying to impose."

But that was exactly what he was doing, he thought as he watched her walk away toward what was presumably a kitchen. She wore jeans and a bulky blue sweatshirt that reached to her hips, with the sleeves pushed up. He would have bet that sweatshirt had belonged to John, and now it was doing double duty as a maternity top.

He stepped into a cozy living room, a collection of aging and mismatched pieces that somehow came together to create a quietly colorful charm. He settled on a goosenecked chair covered with worn burgundy damask, only to pop to his feet again as she returned carrying a glass of milk. She took the other chair, a rocker, probably easier for her to get in and out of these days than the sofa across from them. He sat when she did.

Then the silence grew almost leaden. He let her study him while trying not to return her stare. She hadn't suggested he remove his jacket, so she wanted to keep this short. Fine by him. He could come back tomorrow.

She broke the silence. "You got him the job with the State Department."

If she'd etched the words with acid, they couldn't have stung anymore. "Guilty," he admitted. And of a whole lot more besides.

"Did he know?" she asked.

"Know what?"

"How dangerous it might be?"

God in heaven, that was a question with no right answer. Truth, he decided. As much truth as he could offer. "Yes."

"As dangerous as being in the Rangers?"

Again he offered the truth. "It wasn't supposed to be."

She closed her eyes again, and he noted that she was rocking a little faster. "They won't tell me the truth," she murmured. "They said it was a mugging." Her eyes snapped open. "I know Johnny. No mugger could have taken him."

It was true. But it was equally true that they'd given him the same story. "They told me the same thing. A street mugging." Initially. Unfortunately, he couldn't reveal the little he'd learned later without revealing operational secrets. God, he'd been a fool not to have considered all the secrets he'd have to continue to keep. But still, he owed this woman and her child something.

Her gaze bored into him. "Do you believe it?"

"I...found it difficult. But..." He hesitated, choosing his words carefully. Some things he knew couldn't be shared. Other than that, he knew almost nothing. "Muggings, street violence, in other places...well, they aren't what we know here. And it's pretty bad in some places here."

Her rocking slowed, and he watched tension seep out of her. At last she lifted her milk and sipped it. "So you're as much in the dark as I am."

He chose not to answer.

Then she smiled faintly. "So you're R.T. And here I thought you were an Arthur. Why didn't you ever visit when he was home?"

"Because," he said with perfect truth, "when John came home, all he wanted to do was be with you. I wouldn't have intruded even if he had asked me."

Marisa felt the words burrow straight to her heart like a spike. Reminding her of her loss, a loss that walked beside her every waking minute and during sleep sometimes, as well. But she heard the truth in them. He *had* known Johnny, because once she had suggested that he bring home some of his friends to visit. His answer had been, "I'm selfish. When I'm home I want you all to myself."

She studied this Ryker Tremaine, this ghost out of John's past. She saw in him the same hardness that she had sometimes seen in Johnny. Men who had faced death in the service of a cause. It changed them, gave them an edge.

A tall man, solid, with a face etched by many suns and hardships into a near rocky definition. A square face, with eyes almost like midnight and a strong jaw. He had been pared, the way she had watched Johnny get pared by his experiences. Honed, like fine knives.

Seeing Johnny in him, seeing a resemblance in their characters, eased her doubts even more. She'd invited a stranger in, and now she recognized him. Johnny's ilk. Johnny's friend. Certainly someone who had walked the same difficult, secretive paths.

"Why are you here?" she asked.

"John wanted it. Because…" She watched him hesitate, wondering what he was withholding. "Because I care." That at least sounded true.

"Did he ask you to come?"

Ryker shook his head. "Not exactly. This wasn't supposed to happen. But after he started working at State, yes, he did ask me to check on you. I wasn't sure if he wanted me to come or just call you."

She could believe that. The fist that had been clenching her heart, since she'd realized Ryker was part of Johnny's history, loosened its grip a bit. "I'm sorry," she said. "I don't mean to be cold. It must be hard for you, too."

Something passed quickly over his face, then he said bluntly, "It's been hell. Not your kind of hell, I'm sure, but it's been hell."

She felt a little warmth for him then. Though she hadn't thought much about it, Johnny must have left other people grieving, too. Like an old friend named Ryker Tremaine. "You want to talk about him?"

"If you want to."

"I have some gaps I'd like filled in."

Again that odd hesitation from him, but then he explained, "Within the bounds of operational secrecy. You must have heard that from John."

Words she had come to hate, because they had left her with huge holes in her memory of Johnny. Things she would never know, things he couldn't share. Maybe even some things he didn't want to share, which she could understand. But now, with an empty future in front of her, she was hungry to fill in that unknown past. Things he had done and seen but had never mentioned.

She rocked a little more, feeling her child stirring inside her. She laid her hand over her belly, feeling the active little pokes. A girl. She'd kept that to herself, as well.

"Johnny didn't know we were going to have a baby," she said. One of her greatest pains, laid bare now to a stranger. "I called to tell him, but he wasn't there, and then…"

"I just heard about it recently. Evidently John wasn't the only one who didn't know."

She nodded, absorbing the betrayal again. He should have at least known about his baby before he was killed. It seemed so wrong that he didn't.

"He'd have been happy," Ryker offered.

"I suppose." Another resentment bubbled up inside her, one she tried to bury, but one she couldn't quite quell. "He was gone a lot. Did he tell you how we met?"

"You grew up together."

"Not quite. He was older. A senior in high school when I was in seventh grade. I had a crush on him, but he didn't know it until much, much later. I was in my last year of college when he came home on a visit and noticed me. Really noticed me. We were married the day after I graduated. Then he was off again."

"It was hard on you." It didn't sound like a question.

"Of course. But he laid it all out. I knew what it would be like. What mattered was that we loved each other."

Ryker nodded. "Of course. I know he loved you more than anything on this earth."

She felt her mouth twist. "Not quite. The Rangers were his first love. No competition there."

Ryker surprised her then. He leaned forward, putting his elbows on his knees. "I wouldn't say that. I listened to him talk about you. Man, did he brag when you got your master's degree. When you started teaching at the college here. He was so proud of you."

"I was proud of him, too," she answered simply. "I still am." Then the grief speared her again. "When he took the job with the State Department, I thought he'd be safer!"

"He should have been, Marisa."

Anguish twisted her gut. The baby reacted, kicking hard. "Well, he wasn't."

Ryker didn't answer, not that she could blame him. How did you respond to that? She had no answers for herself, so how could anyone else? She leaned back in the rocker, giving her lungs a little more room, feeling the baby's agitation like scalding criticism. She had to remain calm for her daughter.

Ryker remained silent, a sphinx full of secrets he was no more likely to share than Johnny had been. Why had he come? Because of Johnny? Probably. But to what purpose? What could he possibly do to make any of this better? "I don't see the point of you coming."

"To help in whatever way I can. Just to talk if that's all you want from me. But I'm going to stay in town for a while, Marisa. I know my arrival is a shock, and I'm sorry. But I owe something to John."

"John's past caring," she said bitterly.

"Not for me he isn't. And if there's anything I can do for you, I'll do it, even if it's just knocking down the icicles out front."

She looked at him again and couldn't mistake his determination. Wherever Johnny's loss had forced her, it was clearly pushing this man, too. So they had something in common. Little enough.

She closed her eyes again, rocking gently, feeling her baby settle down, the pokes lessening. Peace returning. A hard-won peace. Acceptance hadn't come easily, but it had come, although it hadn't eased her grief one bit yet.

If there was any blessing in all of this, it was that during her marriage she'd grown accustomed to Johnny's long absences. She didn't expect to see him around every corner, didn't expect to wake to find him beside her in bed, didn't keep listening for the sound of his voice. Not every waking moment prodded her with reminders of his absence.

But the grief, anger and sometimes even despair often rolled over her like a tsunami, irresistible and agonizing. For all the holes in the past, there was a bigger one in the present.

Let it go, just let it go. The man nearby was grieving, too. Maybe together they could find some answers for each other. Not that life offered many answers. Things just seemed to happen.

She looked at Ryker again. He studied his hands, or maybe the floor. She couldn't tell which. "How long will you be in town?"

"I don't know. I *do* know that I'm not leaving immediately. And I have quite a bit of time."

Meaning what, exactly? "So you were with Johnny in the Rangers, too?"

"We worked together on a number of missions."

She accepted that, for now at least. "When he joined the State Department, I thought we'd be traveling a lot. I was looking forward to it. Only he got sent somewhere families can't go."

"I know. There are a lot of those places, unfortunately."

"So what do you do?"

His smile was almost crooked. "Security. Keeping the embassy or consulates safe, and most especially the people who work there."

"Johnny was a translator." But of course he knew that. Her husband had a gift for languages. He soaked them up the way the grass soaked up the rain. She'd never found out exactly how many of them he knew. But then she'd never asked him to count them for her. When they'd been together, other things had seemed so much more important, the sharing and caring and lovemaking. The occasional time with old friends, but mostly... She lifted her head. "Our marriage was like one long honeymoon. When he was home we might as well have been on our own planet."

Ryker's face shadowed. "That's wonderful."

"I thought so. We never had enough time to take one another for granted." Why was she telling him this? Was she reminding herself? Was it important somehow? "But one thing I took for granted was that we'd have a future. No matter where he went, I always believed he'd come home. I was a fool."

"You were an optimist," he corrected firmly. "How else could you do it?"

Good question, she supposed. No answer, but still a good question.

He spoke again. "Some of us do things with our lives that are very unfair to the people we love."

"Are you married?"

He shook his head. "I envied John. He was happy with you, he trusted that you were strong enough to handle all this. I could never trust that much."

"Maybe you were kinder." She hated herself for saying it, but there it was. Johnny had trusted her to be able to handle *this*?

"No, I wasn't kinder," he said. "More selfish. Love 'em and leave 'em, that was me. My romantic past is strewn with ugliness. John at least made a commitment, tried to build something good. I not only envied him, I admired him for it." Then he offered her something approximating a smile. "But then I never met a woman like you."

"Meaning?"

"One who could put up with this. They always wanted me to change. You didn't try to change John. Pretty special."

"Trying to change someone is pointless." Of this she was certain. "We are who we are, and if you can't love someone just the way they are, then you don't love them."

"There's a lot of wisdom in that."

"Just truth." She sighed. Facing up to reality again. Always painful these days. "So you weren't with John when this happened?"

"I was in another country. A little far away to be of any use."

"Johnny could take care of himself," she said. "I guess that's what's bugging me as much as anything. He could take care of himself. This shouldn't have happened."

Ryker stirred. "No, it shouldn't have. But a lot of things shouldn't happen. I live in a world where things that shouldn't happen often do. I'm just sorry you got dragged into it. I'm sorry John didn't make it. I'm sorry as hell I got him the job. And I wish it had been my funeral, not his."

She couldn't doubt him, but this wasn't right. She

felt a stirring of self-disgust. All her dumping had done was make this man feel worse about something that had been out of his control. What kind of shrew was she becoming?

"Don't say that, Ryker. Please. I'm not attacking you."

"Why not? I deserve it. I saw my good friend talking about changing careers, and I found him a job. It's my fault you're grieving, and I know it. I should have just told him to come home to you and become a shopkeeper or something."

That had the oddest effect on her. It booted her right out of her misery to a place where she could actually see some humor. The shift was instantaneous and shocking. She actually laughed. It sounded rusty, but it was real. "Tell me," she said, "do you really think Johnny would have done that? Do you think he'd have taken that job you got him if it wasn't what he really wanted to do? Come on, Ryker. Let's be honest here. Johnny was Johnny, and he'd have made a lousy shopkeeper."

Astonishingly, he smiled. It was a beautiful expression, erasing all the hardness from his face, nearly lighting up the room. Her heart quickened, but she barely noticed. "You're right," he said.

"Of course I'm right. He was an adventurer at heart. I knew it. I walked into it with my eyes open. That's not making this hurt any less, but there was no way I was going to keep him stapled to my side for fifty years. If not this, then something else."

He sat up, half nodding, half shaking his head. "Probably," he agreed, then made an effort to change the subject. "Are you still teaching?"

"I'm on sabbatical until next fall." She paused, then decided her reasoning needn't be kept private. "It felt like too much to deal with—the baby, Johnny's death. I couldn't have focused on teaching. So I decided to focus on getting through this year, having the baby and taking some time to be a mother. Fall will be soon enough."

Soon enough to try to resume a full life. Right now she wanted no part of it. Her life was all in a shambles, and she felt like she had to glue some of the pieces back together before she'd be any use to anyone. She tried to think of it as convalescence. Maybe it was sheer cowardice. An unwillingness to face more of the world than she had to, to deal with constant reminders that life went on. To deal with students who were young enough to be cheerfully falling in love or agonizing over not being asked for a date. For young people, even minor things were magnified. For her, she didn't need a magnifying glass. She doubted she'd have patience for all that. She even doubted whether she'd be focused enough to be a good teacher.

Life had become an unending blur of pain punctuated by moments when she felt the joy of the coming child. A stark contrast that left her feeling continually off balance.

Ryker drew her attention back to him by rising. "I didn't mean to intrude for so long. I just wanted you to know that I'm here. If it's okay, I'll stop by again in the morning."

She didn't move. "Where are you staying?"

"At the motel."

She sighed. "Lovely place."

"I've stayed in worse." He moved toward the door. "Don't see me out. And like I said, I'll stop by in the morning. I don't know about you, but I need some rest. Still adjusting to a major clock change. Jet lag."

She looked up at him. "Where did you fly in from?"

A half smile. "Quite a few time zones to the east. Even more if you count to the west."

A pang struck her. "Johnny used to say something like that. Really helpful."

"I told you…"

She waved a hand. "I get it. Operational security."

He paused and offered his hand. Reluctantly she took it, feeling warm, work-hardened skin. So familiar, but from a stranger. "Ryker…"

"We can talk more tomorrow." He gave her hand a squeeze, then let himself out.

When Marisa heard the front door close, she felt at once a sense of relief and one of disappointment. There was more she wanted to ask. A lot more.

Well, he said he'd come back. Then she sat rocking and thinking about Ryker Tremaine. She didn't quite trust him, even if he had been Johnny's friend. How could she? He wouldn't give her any more answers than her husband had.

Men who lived in the shadows, both of them. After all these years she was just beginning to understand how much.

Finally she rose, rubbing her back a bit, and went to lock the front door, something she didn't usually do.

But the simple fact was, a stranger had come to her door, claiming to know Johnny. Maybe he did, but that alone didn't make him trustworthy.

In all, the situation felt wrong. After all these months? Out of the blue without warning? Not even a condolence card? While she wasn't yet prepared to reject the possibility that he was the "Artie" Johnny had sometimes mentioned, even that alone wasn't enough to create trust.

He was a stranger. And while she might not care all that much about her own life, she *did* care about her baby.

When at last she went to bed, she rested on her side, feeling her daughter's gentle stirrings, and staring into the darkness. She thought of Johnny, which was slowly growing easier, she thought about the child who would soon join her in this world and she thought about Ryker Tremaine.

Her sense of him was that he was a lot like Johnny in some ways. But different, too. Maybe even harder.

Or maybe this visit had been as difficult for him as it had been for her. She couldn't imagine why he was planning to stay, was troubled by the fact that he wouldn't say for how long, and realized that another box of secrets had just walked into her life.

Like she needed more of that. At last sleep freed her, giving her gentle dreams for a change, offering escape from a world that had too many hard edges.

Morning would come. Somehow, to her everlasting sorrow, it always did.

Chapter Two

Rising before the sun. The phrase had amused Marisa since childhood, especially since she was climbing out of bed at the same time as usual. The sun's winter-delayed arrival always made her feel cozy somehow, and this morning was no different. By the time she finished showering and dressing in one of Johnny's old flannel shirts and maternity jeans, faint gray light began to appear around the edges of the curtains.

In the kitchen she made her allotted few cups of coffee and decided to eat cinnamon oatmeal for breakfast. With a glass of milk, she swallowed her prenatal vitamin while she stirred the oatmeal.

She had just poured the oatmeal from the pan into the bowl when she heard a knock at her side door. Looking over, she saw Julie standing there and waving. Immediately she went to let her in.

"Gawd, it's cold out there this morning," Julie said, pulling back her hood and shaking out her long auburn hair. Green eyes danced. "Be glad you don't have to be anywhere. After that thaw last week, it feels like an insult. Oatmeal, huh?"

"Want me to make you some?"

"Sweetie, I already gorged on Danish and coffee. Unlike you, I don't have to worry about healthy eating."

Marisa laughed lightly. "Not yet, anyway."

"I know, I know, it'll catch up with me. All our sins do. So, dish."

"Dish?"

Julie pulled out a chair without unzipping her jacket and sat, arching a brow at her. "Did you really think a mysterious man could show up on your doorstep last evening and that your neighbor Fiona would miss it? Or that she wouldn't call me and probably half the rest of the town? Sit, eat."

Marisa brought the bowl of oatmeal and a milky mug of coffee to the table. Julie eyed the coffee. "Still on restriction?"

Marisa shook her head. "Not now. The doc says I can have more, it's not risky. But now…I don't want any more."

"Hah. They retrain us. Anyway, the guy last night."

"Fiona. Does she report on every breath I take?"

"You know her better than that. But last night was something new. Everyone needs something new to talk about. So, who was he?" Julie waited eagerly.

"He says he worked with Johnny for years."

Julie's smile faded. "What's wrong, Marisa? Did he scare you?"

"I don't know what to make of him, that's all. He said

a few things, so yes he knew Johnny but…it seems kind of late to be making a social call. He certainly doesn't know me. And he's talking about Johnny wanting him to check on me."

"Well, that sounds like Johnny."

Marisa's head popped up, a spoonful of oatmeal in her hand. "What do you mean by that?"

Julie bit her lip, finally shrugged and said, "Johnny asked me to keep an eye on you if… Well, you get it."

"He did?" Anger billowed in Marisa. "He asked you that, and you never told me?"

Julie put up a hand. "He asked me not to. Don't bite my head off. But, frankly, I could see his point."

Marisa put down her spoon and gripped the edge of the table. "See what point?"

"The point that he was going away for months at a time to do a dangerous job, and sometimes his feet touched ground long enough to worry about *you*. He didn't want to share that with you because you might worry about him more. It was always understood, wasn't it, that Johnny would come home?"

The oatmeal was beginning to congeal. Marisa pushed it to the side, her appetite utterly gone. More secrets, now one that had been shared with her best friend. What else hadn't Johnny told her? She guessed at some of it, but now she wondered. "What else?"

"That was it," Julie answered quietly. "You know Johnny. He made light of it when he asked me, but I could tell he was serious. I'd have looked after you, anyway. You're my best friend."

Numbness was slowly replacing anger. Julie popped up. "Let me make you some fresh oatmeal."

"I don't want it anymore. Maybe I'll make some later."

Julie paused beside her, squeezing her shoulder. "I didn't mean to upset you. I honestly didn't think that telling you that would."

"No?" Craning her neck, Marisa looked up at her. "How many other things didn't he tell me?"

"God," Julie breathed. Slowly she returned to her chair. "Don't take it like that. We all know he couldn't talk about his work. It wasn't like he was running around confiding in everyone except you. That was it, Marisa, I swear. Given that he had a dangerous job, why should it surprise anyone that he asked a handful of close people to help you out if something went wrong? Seems more thoughtful than secretive to me."

Maybe Julie was right. Gripping her mug in both hands, Marisa tried to swallow the coffee before it cooled down too much and warmed her not at all. But this on the heels of last night…she felt alarm flags popping up inside her. Had she ever known her husband at all?

"Damn it," Julie muttered. "The last thing on earth I wanted to do was make you feel bad. I just came over to hear about Mr. Mysterious, and look what I've done."

Marisa didn't answer immediately. Julie had been her friend since kindergarten, and she had to believe her. So Johnny had been worried. Well, he'd kind of explained the possibility when they were dating. He'd been in the Rangers, after all. Going into combat and who knew what else. She certainly didn't. How would anything have changed if he'd told her he'd asked friends to check on her if something happened? Not at all. She would still have moved forward with the certainty that he would always return, because any other possibility was unthinkable. Johnny had seemed to believe that himself. Maybe she was more troubled by the realization that he'd been acutely aware that he might not come back. If so, he hadn't shared that with her. Another in his long line of omissions, most of which hadn't bothered her. So why was this getting to her?

"So," Julie said eventually, "I've got only a few minutes before I have to get to work. I want to hear about this friend of Johnny's."

Marisa struggled back to the present moment. "Not much to say. He's in town for a few days. He wanted to see how I was doing mainly because Johnny asked him to at one time or another."

"But it took him six months to get here?"

Marisa nodded. "Same kind of job as Johnny's. Anyway, I gather from what he said that he heard I was pregnant and that galvanized him to get here. He said something about how Johnny had mentioned that I was safe here, among friends. So maybe it didn't seem all that critical."

"Or," Julie said fairly, "he simply couldn't get away."

"Maybe."

"So…" Julie grinned. "Is he gorgeous?"

"Julie!" Marisa's shock caused her to gasp. "Are you kidding?"

"No, perfectly serious. Johnny wouldn't want you to bury yourself, and a calendar is a poor way to measure grief. I always thought that old thing about wearing widows weeds for a year was a bit over the top. I mean, you grieve however long you grieve. There's not some magic date when it stops. As for everything else—" she pushed back from the table and stood "—you're still here, hon. You should snap at anything good that happens by, or the next fifty years are going to be awful. At least enjoy having a new face around for a few days. I'm off!"

Anything good that happens by? Really? Emotionally she still felt like a train wreck most of the time. Snap at life? The only snapping she'd like to do was angry.

Then her baby stirred again, reminding her she did indeed have to carry on. She scraped the oatmeal into the trash and made herself a fresh bowl to eat with her second cup of coffee.

Slowly, as the warm oatmeal and coffee hit her system, calm began to settle over her. When she was done eating, she sat for a while with her eyes closed, her hands on her belly, and concentrated on the new life growing inside her.

She already loved her child. It hadn't taken long for that to happen. At first, during the darkest days, she'd hated her pregnancy almost as if it were a promise that would never be fulfilled. She'd gone through the motions of taking care of herself only because she had to. But then had come the day when she had felt the first movement. Even in the midnight of her soul, she'd felt an incredible burst of joy, a connection she had never imagined possible before she even saw the child. Her baby was growing inside her, and it was indeed a promise. Her child, her love. An unbreakable link was forged with those first tiny, almost bubble-like movements.

The future *did* hold something good, she reminded herself. It held this baby, Johnny's final gift, a new life she needed to live for and work for. A purpose, a joy, a journey. Her imaginings might have turned to dust with Johnny, but now there were new imaginings. Maybe it was time to quit fighting with herself and just get on with setting up the nursery, making sure she had everything a baby would need. Maybe it was time to accept Julie's repeated offer of a baby shower. Time to stiffen her spine and start taking steps of her own choice into all the tomorrows to come.

Because if she was sure of anything, it was that she couldn't remain like this, paralyzed and hunkered down. If she didn't change it now, she'd be changing it in a few months because life would force it on her.

Maybe it was time to stop being a victim.

The doorbell rang shortly after she finished washing her breakfast dishes and absently wiping the counters clean. Ryker, she thought. No one else she knew in Conard City would come by at this time of day. She'd half expected never to see him again. She hadn't been exactly welcoming last night, and he could have called his duty to Johnny done. He'd checked on her. What more could Johnny have expected of him, of a man who was a stranger to her?

She dried her hands on a towel, smoothed her still-damp hair back quickly, then went to answer the door. She half hoped it was Fiona, who lived next door, coming to try to pry some more gossip out of her. Fiona, she often thought, needed to get a job now that her two children spent all day in school. She clearly didn't have enough to do with her time. Of course, who was Marisa to criticize anyone else for that?

But as she had half feared, she opened the door to see Ryker. He looked more rested, his face less like granite this morning. Sunlight reflected almost blindingly off the snow.

"Good morning," he said pleasantly. He offered a small white bag. "Bagels from your local bakery. I figured they couldn't be too bad for you. Want me to knock down those icicles?"

She felt as if a whirlwind had just blown into her quiet life. "The icicles are really bothering you," she remarked, suddenly remembering that he'd mentioned them last night.

He glanced over his shoulder. "Most of them aren't too dangerous, but why let them grow? Got a broomstick?"

Arguing seemed utterly pointless. She gave him her broom, then listened to the dull thuds from the porch as he took down the icicles. In the kitchen, she opened the bag he'd brought, and her nose immediately filled with the amazing smell of oven-fresh bagels. For the first time that morning, she became genuinely hungry. Melinda, the bakery owner, had also tossed in a few small containers of cream cheese. At that point it seemed churlish not to set out a couple of plates and make some fresh coffee.

Ryker came in, bringing the cold and the broom with him. "All done. Where should I put this?"

She pointed to the pantry door at the back of the kitchen. "Just inside there. Thank you."

"Safety, that's my thing," he said as he put the broom away and shucked his jacket, revealing a gray flannel shirt that made his eyes and hair look even darker. "How are you this morning?"

"I'm okay." It was the best she could say. "I made coffee to go with the bagels. Do you drink it?"

"By the gallon. But you don't have to feed me just because—"

She interrupted him, feeling a sense of desperation. "Let's get past this, okay? Maybe you showed up out of nowhere without any warning. Maybe I don't know you from Adam, but you're here because of Johnny. One way or another we should both respect his wishes. He wanted you to check on me. I'm not going to tell you to get lost, at least not right away. You brought breakfast, which was nice, and I do have enough manners left to invite you to enjoy it with me. Okay?"

For a couple of seconds he didn't move, then a smile spread slowly. "Cutting to the chase, huh?"

"As much as I can. We can spend the next few hours fencing around, but honestly, I hate wasting time like that. Especially now. Sit down. Eat. I'll join you. Thank you for the bagels."

With a snort like a laugh, he took the chair she indicated at the kitchen table. The bagels were already sliced, so all they had to do was spread the cream cheese. Melinda, the bakery owner, had remembered that Marisa liked hers with chives. She hadn't had room to feel much outside her own pained universe for the past few months, but she was touched now by Melinda's thoughtfulness. So many good people around here, and she'd been avoiding most of them.

Maybe Ryker's arrival had jarred her out of her self-preoccupation. Was grief selfish? She supposed it was.

At least he didn't tell her to sit while he got the coffee, or otherwise imply that she wasn't perfectly healthy. Lately, on the rare occasions she visited with her friends, they wanted her to let them take care of everything, as if she were an invalid. She understood they felt helpless to do much about anything else, but really, she was in good health and capable of getting a cup of coffee for someone.

But then the awkwardness returned. Ryker decided to pierce it. "I probably know more about you than you do about me," he remarked. "Johnny talked about you from time to time, but I gather he said little about me."

"He mentioned R.T. a couple of times, but, no, he didn't say much. But then he didn't talk much about his friends in the Rangers or later. It was like when he came home, he turned all that off."

"Probably wise," Ryker said. He washed down a mouthful of bagel with some coffee. "Compartmentalizing, we call it. Keeping things separate. Why would he want to bring any of that home to you?"

"But he talked about me," she argued.

"Once in a while. Sometimes everyone talked about home. Sometimes we needed to remember that there was a place or a person we wanted to get back to. The rest of the time we couldn't afford the luxury."

That hit her hard, but she faced it head-on. Remembering home had been a luxury? That might have been the most important thing anyone had told her about what Johnny had faced and done.

"I didn't know him at all," she whispered, squeezing her eyes shut, once again feeling the shaft of pain.

"You knew the best part of him. That mattered to him, Marisa. You gave him a place where that part could flourish."

"But why?" she asked, opening her eyes. "Why do you get into this? This kind of life?"

"I can't speak for Johnny. Only for myself."

"Then tell me."

"I was young, hotheaded and determined to do something important with my life. And in case you start to wonder, Johnny did a lot of very important things. But we don't know what it'll cost when we cross the line and take up the work. We have no idea in hell what we're getting into. No one can."

She managed a stiff nod and tried to eat some more

bagel. The baby kicked, then she felt a little foot or hand trail slowly along her side.

"Anyway," Ryker continued after finishing half a bagel, "we do it for a variety of reasons. I wanted excitement. Exotic places. A sense of mission and purpose. Adrenaline junkie, I guess."

"And Johnny?"

Ryker spread his hand. "By the time I met him, I couldn't have guessed a thing about why. By then he was one of us. And as you so correctly said last night, by then he wouldn't have been happy with a tamer life. Somehow, I guess that's how we're built." He frowned faintly and looked past her. "I don't know if I can make you understand, or even find the right words. But there's a point where the mission becomes everything. It motivates every breath we take. Not for everyone, mind you. But for some of us…well, we get hooked. We don't just carry the sword, we *are* the sword." He shrugged and picked up another piece of bagel. "Unfortunately, the world needs swords. I'd have made a lousy plowshare, I guess."

The reference didn't escape her. Her stomach turned over, and for a few seconds she felt so nauseated she wondered if she'd have to run to the bathroom.

But memories floated back, instants out of time, just brief things she had heard or seen with Johnny, moments when he had seemed almost like someone else. Moments when she glimpsed the sword. They always passed swiftly, wiped away by a ready smile, but she'd seen them. She just hadn't wanted to remember them.

But recalling them now, she felt just awful that Johnny had felt the need to hide a very big part of himself from her. She'd have loved him no matter what. Hadn't he trusted her?

"We also get older," Ryker continued. "So we change some more. I'm nearly forty. Too damn old for this business. Johnny was starting to feel the same way. So after I moved over to State, he asked me to let him know if something opened up."

"How could you give up the rush?"

Another faint smile. Her insides prickled with unwanted awareness of him as a man. She shoved it quickly aside, and guilt replaced it. At least he was speaking.

"It's possible to get one without being the pointy tip of the sword. Besides, it's important to know when the time has come. You can shift without giving up the mission or your sense of purpose. It's safer for everyone. Johnny had started to think more about you, about being with you more."

Her breath caught. "He told you that?"

"Actually, yes. When he asked me to let him know if there was a position for him, he said it, Marisa. He said he was thinking about all the time he'd missed being with you, and that he was ready to start down a different road. Unfortunately…"

"Yes," she said tightly. Unfortunately. Johnny had said the same thing when he told her was trying to get a job with the State Department. *We'll have more time together. We'll even be able to travel together once in a while. I'll need to work my way up a little higher on the food chain, but think of the places we could visit.*

How much of that had been real? "Just last night you said he knew it could be dangerous."

"It's always dangerous," Ryker said bluntly. "Always. But I didn't think it would get him killed."

Nor had she. In her blissful ignorance, she had forgotten all the places in the world where a State Department employee would be unwelcome. No, she'd been thinking of London, Paris, Tokyo…not little out-of-the-way consulates in dangerous countries. But of course Johnny wouldn't shy away from the dangers. He never had.

She needed to get away from this, at least for now. Ryker was shifting her mental images around like a puzzle, and she wasn't sure she would like the new picture. "So, more about you," she said.

"I was born," he said.

Despite everything, she felt her mood rising to a much lighter place, and realized she desperately needed it. "That's it?" she asked, surprised to hear a tremor of humor in her voice.

"No, of course that's not it. I had, still have, family. I grew up like a normal kid, two parents and a sister. My parents are retired now, and my sister lives in New Zealand. I get to see her once every few years. And that's where normal ended, I guess. The military called to me like a siren. My imaginings were very different from reality. But I think I mentioned that. Anyway, since then my home has been my job."

None of that told her very much, but what had she been expecting? "That could be lonely."

"I haven't noticed it, except occasionally." The way he spoke led her to believe there had been times when it had been incredibly lonely. She wondered if Johnny had felt that way sometimes, too. And why.

"So you're going back to teaching in the fall?"

She nodded. "I hope I'm ready by then. I'd be a lousy teacher right now."

"How are you filling your days?"

"Trying to get through them."

The words lay there, stark and revealing. More than she had wanted to say to this stranger, more than she had even said to her friends. The fact that hell lived inside her was not something she felt compelled to inflict on her friends. She tried to keep it to herself as much as humanly possible. She knew she didn't do the best job of it, but she still made the effort.

"Everything's okay with the baby, though?"

"Fine." It wasn't really his business.

"And a nursery? Have you put one together?"

She felt a prickle of guilt. Her pregnant friends had usually attacked the nursery business early and had things ready months in advance. For some reason she had been postponing it, as if she could stay in this state of stasis forever. Unrealistic. Ducking. Evading what she couldn't have said. "No. There's a crib in the basement that was Johnny's. I thought I'd use that."

"Need help getting it up here?"

It was clear he wanted to do something more than knock down a few icicles. Well, this was one task where help would be welcome. "Yes, actually I do."

She had just given him a wedge to drive farther into her life. She hoped like hell she didn't regret it.

Glad of a useful job to do, Ryker headed downstairs to the basement. Marisa had told him where to find the crib, and he didn't have any trouble locating it. The basement was clean, scrupulously organized and stocked with every tool a man could wish for. The only thing that bothered him was that the laundry machines were down here. That meant Marisa was going up and down those narrow steps at least once a week, and when the baby came she'd have to do them even more often. He didn't like it. The railing didn't seem stout enough; the steps were too narrow. How often would she attempt them with a baby in her arms? He hated to think.

But as he carried the awkwardly sized pieces of the crib frame up one by one, he had the opportunity to think about Johnny and Marisa, and his opinion was changing.

Had Johnny even once considered how his death would gut his wife? Had he ever looked at her and wondered what would become of her? In just a short time Ryker had gleaned a decent impression of the price Marisa was paying, a price compounded by the impending arrival of a child she would now have to care for on her own. He had no doubt she could do it, but there'd be no handy dad to spell her when she got tired or needed a break.

Lots of women did it. He got it. But Marisa should have had Johnny to lean on. Of course, Johnny had been so busy pursuing his new goals that maybe he'd have been no help at all.

Thoughts such as these had been one of the main reasons Ryker had avoided every opportunity to settle down. It wasn't just that women wanted to change him. No, they had a right to expect certain things from a husband, things he couldn't provide.

And the lie. The big lie. That they would travel together? Johnny would likely have never been assigned to any station where he could take his family. Not with his skills.

And another lie, his own. He and Johnny didn't work for the State Department. They worked for the CIA. State was their cover. He hated having to perpetuate that with Marisa. At this point she deserved something better than lies. She certainly deserved to know about a black star on a marble wall at Langley that would never bear Johnny's name.

But the simple fact was, the agency would put up the star, but it might never acknowledge that John had been one of them. It had happened before and would happen again, and setting Marisa on a quest to break through that huge barrier to truth seemed fruitless. Some names were never inscribed in the book, which was guarded as well as the crown jewels. Some families were never invited to the annual memorial ceremony. Some were never told what their loved ones had done. Some were left forever with stories such as those Marisa had been told because even one slip might cause an irreparable harm.

He didn't even know himself exactly what had happened to John. He'd never know. But he didn't like giving her the cover story when she deserved the truth.

But maybe the truth would upset her more. Maybe knowing that all that talk about exotic travel had been most likely lies would only compound sins that never seemed to stop compounding.

He'd been at this business longer than John had; he was more used to deceptions that went with it. But he found himself getting sick to the gills of it. That woman up there reminded him that secrecy had repercussions. Horrible repercussions. At least if John had been killed in a combat mission with the Rangers, she'd have been given some information about where, when and how that was truthful. Instead, she'd been given a lie. A street mugging?

Not much closure, especially when she was right that John could have taken care of himself.

He brought the springs up to the bedroom she had indicated. Her room, he guessed, at the back of the house. She wanted the child near. She was already working over the wood with a damp rag. He looked at the springs, though, and wondered if they should be replaced. A few rusty spots marred them.

"Can we get new springs for the crib?" We, as if he belonged.

She let it pass, though, and stepped over to look. "Maybe I should."

"Can you get them in town?"

"I can order them. I know I need to order a mattress."

But not a whole new crib. He didn't need brilliant insight to understand that. "Let me measure them, then. Can you just call to order them?"

"Freitag's?" She smiled faintly. "They'll order anything anyone around here wants. We used to have a catalog store, but that closed. Miracle of the internet."

"Where do I find a tape measure?"

He found it in the kitchen drawer she had directed him to and returned with it and the memo pad and pen from the fridge. He measured the frame, made notes about how it bolted to the bed, then joined her in wiping down the wood. At last she sat on the edge of her bed, holding her stomach and laughed. "That felt good!"

"Yeah? Somehow I think you need to tell that to your back."

"How did you guess?"

"Because mine would have been aching after being bent over all that time." He stepped back and looked at the crib. "It's a very nice piece of furniture."

"Johnny's grandfather built it for him. Carpentry was his hobby."

"A great heirloom then." He looked again at the springs. "You know, I should probably take this back downstairs and work on it with some oil and rust remover. Maybe it doesn't need to be replaced."

She shook her head. "I want new springs if I can get them. Babies bounce when they get old enough to stand. I wouldn't trust it."

"Fair enough," he agreed, and carted it back down to the basement. He could also put some wood slats in place to replace the springs, he thought. Peg them in so they couldn't slip out.

But why was he even thinking of such things? He had no place here, and no sense of how long Marisa would tolerate him. Worse, with every passing hour he was building the wall of lies higher.

Sometimes he just hated himself.

When he got back upstairs, he found Marisa in the kitchen. She was nibbling on some carrots, and a plate of them sat at the center of the table as if in invitation to him.

"Mind if I get some coffee?" he asked.

"Help yourself. Make fresh if you want. And thanks for your help with the crib."

"No big deal." He filled a mug and sat across from her. She appeared pensive, so he waited for her to speak.

"You know, I don't want to use springs in that crib at all. I shouldn't need them. They look dangerous to me, and my friends all have mattresses that just sit on brackets around the outside of the crib."

He summoned a mental picture. "That would work.

I could add some more brackets for you easily enough. The way it looks now, you only have four of them."

She nodded thoughtfully. "I'd need them all the way around so the mattress is higher. You know, so fingers or hands couldn't poke out."

"Easy enough."

Then she smiled faintly. "And that's part of the reason for crib bumpers, I guess." A little shake of her head. "I need to get on the stick about this, don't I?"

"You've got a little time."

"Not a whole lot." She held out her hand. "Pad? Pen?"

He'd forgotten he'd tucked them into his breast pocket and turned them over immediately.

"So, hardware for angle brackets and screws, right? Say eight of them?"

"Maybe twelve. And they should be wide, not too narrow."

She wrote. "Then mattress, bumpers, sheets, blankets…" Her voice trailed off. "I let this go too long."

"You've still got time, right?"

"Another ten weeks."

"That's plenty," he said bracingly. "Your friends and I will help if you let us." Then he took a leap into a potential briar patch. "I don't like those basement stairs of yours."

She looked up from her writing. "Why?"

"Too narrow, and the railing isn't sturdy enough. "You shouldn't be climbing them right now, but with a baby in your arms or on your hip…" He let it hang, and braced for her justifiable anger. Just who the hell did he think he was? She'd have every right to demand that of him.

She frowned, then sighed. "You're right. I hate those stairs."

"I can fix them."

At that her head jerked back. "Ryker, you just dropped by to do your duty to Johnny. You checked on me. Are you planning to move in?"

A justified question. But he was feeling a need, a strong need to atone and make up for things, including the lies he kept telling by omission as much as anything. His answer, though, surprised even him. "For a change I'd like to actually build something."

Something passed over her face—whether sorrow or something else, he wasn't sure. "Why should I trust you?" she asked finally. "You think I can't tell you're keeping secrets?"

"John kept secrets, too," he said. "And by the way, John trusted me, or I wouldn't be here now."

She debated. He could see it. He wondered how much faith she'd lost in her husband just by the few things he'd told her. He'd certainly tried to avoid telling her that she'd been fed some outright lies. He didn't feel good about it, but that was the job. Besides, he owed it to John to protect her from the ugly truths.

"What would you do to the stairs?" she asked.

"For one thing, the steps need to be wider. So it'll stretch farther into the basement, but there's room. And I'd give you a rail on both sides strong enough that if you grab or fall against them, they won't collapse."

She nodded slowly, giving him his first sense that he might actually be getting somewhere with her. "I'd like that," she admitted.

He rose and reached for the jacket he'd slung over the

back of the chair earlier. "I've imposed too much. See you tomorrow."

Before she could answer, he headed for the door. Coming here hadn't eased his sense of guilt in the least. He'd better watch his step before he carried that woman into another thicket of lies, a thicket worse than the one left to her by John.

He was, after all, still CIA. And while he might have a few months off, that didn't mean he should spend them weaving another trap for an innocent woman. She'd paid a high enough price already for loving the wrong man.

Chapter Three

Ryker's departure left Marisa feeling adrift again. Maybe she'd been too quick to take such a long sabbatical. No, she couldn't have handled teaching in the fall, but now that months had passed, she itched at times to have a schedule, to have things that needed doing. A point, a purpose, beyond wallowing in grief and taking care of her health and the child in her womb.

Johnny's death had inalterably changed her life, but she had managed his absences before by keeping a busy, full life. These days she'd all but cut off her friends.

And Ryker. He intrigued her. She felt the hardness in him at times, but she felt more there. As if he were reaching out for something, too. He'd helped her with the crib, and he said he wanted to fix her basement stairs. God, she hated those stairs. For years now she'd stood at the top of them and thrown her laundry down because she couldn't safely carry it.

It would be nice to get them fixed, but his words had struck her even more: Ryker had said he wanted to *build something for a change*. If that wasn't one of the saddest statements she'd ever heard...

He'd said he handled security for the State Department. She wondered if that job was even more dangerous than Johnny's. Johnny, after all, had gone as a translator. But Ryker being involved in security sounded even more hazardous. Yet he seemed to accept those kinds of risks casually, which was chilling, in a way.

But then, hadn't Johnny done the same?

She tried to fight the downward spiral her thoughts were taking again. Reality decreed she had to carry on. Indulging a grief that would never leave her didn't seem to get her anywhere. One foot in front of the other. How many times had she reminded herself of that?

Julie showed up again in the late afternoon, an unusual number of visits for one day. Apparently Julie was concerned about something. Her? Ryker's presence?

Anyway, it was a relief to see her cheerful face breeze into the house. Julie had apparently taken the bit between her teeth. While she gabbed humorously about her day with "those imps," as she sometimes referred to her kindergarten class, she dove into the refrigerator and started pulling out food.

"I didn't want to eat alone," she remarked. "You up to a chicken casserole?"

"Absolutely." Marisa sat back, enjoying Julie's minor whirlwind.

"Just us, or will your new friend be here?"

"I'm not expecting him."

Julie paused, package of skinless chicken breasts in hand. "Why not? Did he leave?"

"I doubt it. He wants to rebuild my basement stairs."

"I love him already. Those things have been worrying me. So call him."

"Call him? Why?"

"Because in this case three might be company. I mean, sheesh, Marisa, the guy came to look you up because of Johnny. How rude do you want to be?"

Marisa felt her stomach lurch. What was Julie doing? Was she being rude? She hadn't asked Ryker to come visit; he'd just arrived without warning. She didn't owe him a thing...or did she?

"He helped bring the crib upstairs," she said slowly.

"Good man. So you're finally facing the inevitability. Great. And that means we can throw a baby shower for you. My gosh, girl, the presents have already been bought. We've just been waiting for you to agree. And if you don't, you're going to have the shower around your hospital bed. So don't you think it'd be best to know what you already have before you start shopping?"

Marisa felt an urge to giggle rising in the pit of her stomach. "You sound manic."

"Comes from dealing with five-year-olds. Can't keep their attention for long. Talking rapidly is necessary. You never noticed before?"

"I guess not."

Julie rolled her eyes. "Call the man. He must be at the motel. Besides, I want to size him up. Protective urges also go with being a teacher."

And a friend, Marisa thought. But Julie had leavened her mood, and she decided she wouldn't at all mind hearing Julie's opinion of Ryker. Right now she herself couldn't make up her mind about the man. He'd zoomed in from nowhere, and experience with Johnny had taught her that he'd zoom away again just as unexpectedly, and probably without any explanation except he had to return to work. She also wondered if Julie would sense the secretiveness in him, would also feel that Ryker was withholding important information.

Because, honestly, she didn't quite trust the man, whatever his association with Johnny.

Julie left the food on the counter and got them both some coffee. Sitting at the table with her felt good and familiar. "Call him," she said more gently. "A second opinion is good and, frankly, I've been wondering about him all day. Strangers make me uneasy. So let's sort it out."

With an almost leaden hand, Marisa reached for the wall phone and called the motel. One click, and then a voice answered. "Ryker Tremaine."

"Ryker, it's Marisa. My friend Julie and I wondered if you want to join us at my house for dinner. Nothing fancy, just chicken casserole."

Julie grabbed the phone from her hand. "Hi, Ryker, this is Julie. Believe me, my chicken casserole is fancy. Say an hour? We can chat while it cooks. Thanks. Looking forward to it."

Then Julie hung up the phone.

"Why did you do that?" Marisa demanded. She may have been living in a state of near paralysis for months now, but she was still capable of making a phone call.

"Because," Julie said frankly, "you sounded like you didn't want him to come."

"Maybe I don't!"

"Too late now." Julie grinned. "I'm going to get you out of that shell before it hardens into an unbreakable habit. Anyway, I need to start cubing the chicken."

Marisa's curiosity overwhelmed her irritation. It always did with Julie. "What did he say? Did he hesitate?"

"No hesitation. Just asked for time to shower since he was out running."

Marisa's gaze drifted to the window, still frosty in many places. "In this?"

"The tough get going," Julie tossed back as she rose and pulled out the cutting board. "Did you exercise today?"

"I forgot." The realization shocked her. What had happened to the entire day? Had she just sat here brooding for all these hours?

"Bad girl. If you want to ride your exercise bike while I cook, go for it."

Marisa had a recumbent bike to ride every day. It had become too risky to walk outside with patches of ice scattered everywhere, and the bike was designed so that she could lean back and leave plenty of room for her belly. "No. One day off won't kill me."

"Probably not, but you know what the doc said. More exercise means easier labor."

"Like he knows for sure."

Julie giggled. "It's got to be better, and you know it. For bunches of reasons. But you're right, one day off won't kill you. Now enjoy your cup of coffee and watch me slave after a long day of sitting in chairs that are way too small for me and listening to piping voices that never quiet down unless I roll out the nap mats."

However Julie talked about it, Marisa was certain that she loved teaching kindergarten. She'd had a chance to change grades more than once, but she stuck with her five-year-olds.

"Formative years," Julie had explained once, but

Marisa had always believed that Julie got a kick out of the little ones. She also believed that getting them young gave her the best chance to instill a joy in learning. "Not that some other teacher won't knock it out of them," she had added wryly. "But I can't do anything about that. All I can do is give them the best start."

"Well, they've sure lost their interest by the time they get to me," Marisa had retorted.

"That's your fault," Julie had answered. "You should have majored in something besides the classics and dead gods."

Much to her surprise, Marisa felt her mood elevating. Having dinner with Julie and Ryker might well be enjoyable, especially since Julie never pulled her punches.

But the instant she felt her spirits improve, she felt guilty, and her thoughts tried to return to Johnny and his death. For the first time, it occurred to her that she shouldn't feel guilty every time she enjoyed something. In her heart of hearts, she knew Johnny wouldn't have wanted that. She shouldn't want it, either. Grieving was hard enough without adding guilt to the mix every time she knew a few moments of respite from the loss. Julie was right, fifty years was too long to waste.

So she pushed the guilt down and focused instead on the here and now. Julie been trying to tell her for some time that there was no proper way to grieve, no set of requirements to be met. Her heart had been ripped wide open, but that didn't mean she couldn't allow herself to heal.

Locking herself in a permanent purgatory helped no one. It didn't bring Johnny back, and it wouldn't be fair to her baby. Time for some stiff upper lip.

"I was thinking it's time to shop for the baby," she remarked as Julie began to scoop chicken and vegetables into the casserole.

"I saw the list on the fridge. About time, kiddo. But first we'll have the shower. Friday evening. Then I can go shopping with you on Saturday. Or if you really want to splurge, we can go to Casper or Denver. It might do you some good to get away."

Indeed it might. "You're the best, Julie."

"I know." Julie flashed a grin over her shoulder. "The world spins because of me."

Marisa actually laughed. That made two laughs in one day. Maybe she was improving.

Ryker arrived just as Julie was popping the casserole into the oven and setting a timer. "I'll get it," she said when the bell rang. "I want a first view all to myself."

"Do you want a spear and shield, too?" Marisa tried to joke.

"My tongue can take care of all that. Just relax."

Marisa listened to the greetings at the door and thought it all sounded pleasant enough. Julie apparently gave Ryker time to doff his jacket and gloves in the hall, then the two of them returned to the kitchen. She didn't feel tension between them, but somehow she didn't think that would last. She knew Julie too well.

Once they were all seated around the wooden table, Julie plunged right into the inquisition. "So what took you so long to get here?"

Ryker arched one brow. "Meaning?"

"Well, the funeral was nearly six months ago. Most planes are faster than that."

Marisa battled an urge to quell Julie, realizing that she needed to hear some of this, too. And count on Julie to address it baldly.

Ryker rested his arms on the table. He wore a gray
Yale sweatshirt that looked as if it had seen a lot of wash-
ings. "It depends on whether we can take a break," he
answered. "I couldn't get away. Not then."

"But six months?"

Marisa felt this was a bit unfair. She opened her
mouth to say so, but Ryker spoke first. "Sometimes one
is in a situation that one can't walk away from. Not even
for the death of a family member."

"Now that's mysterious," Julie popped back. "I guess
it'll stay that way, won't it?"

"I'm afraid so. There are things I can't talk about.
Marisa knows that. There were things Johnny couldn't
talk about, either."

"I get it," Julie said pleasantly enough. "So, what happened to Johnny? And how about a truthful version?"

Relax? Julie had told her to relax and now she was
delving into this? Marisa wanted to get up and leave,
but Julie had arranged her chair so that Marisa couldn't.
Damn!

"I was told the same thing Marisa was. That's all I
know."

"Officially, anyway," Julie said bluntly. "I guess that's
all anyone will know."

Then Ryker surprised Marisa by getting angry. He'd
seemed so self-contained until that moment, but a definite edge crept into his voice, and his dark eyes sparked.
"That's more than some people get, Julie. Some never
know anything at all." He started to push back from the
table, but Julie's hand shot out and caught him by the
arm. He looked at her grip on him, and Marisa was sure
he could have shaken it away like a fly.

"I'm sorry," Julie said. "I'm worried about Marisa.

She's my friend, and you popped up out of nowhere at a very late date."

Ryker turned his gaze on Marisa. "You couldn't have asked me this yourself? You needed someone else to speak for you?"

"I asked you last night," she reminded him, her heart thumping. He appeared to relax a hair, and Julie released his arm.

"Look," he said, "I didn't come here to make your life harder. I came because John asked me to. I came as soon as I could get away. But if it'll save you problems, I can leave right now. I'd feel bad about it, because I said I'd be here for you, but if you don't want me around, then it hardly matters what I promised."

Before Marisa decided how to answer, Julie looked between them, then said, "We're throwing Marisa a baby shower on Friday night. You can crash it if you want. Of course you might get nauseated looking at tiny clothes and booties."

Several noticeable seconds passed before Ryker answered. Marisa got the distinct impression that he was putting a lid on something inside himself, although she couldn't imagine whether it was anger or sorrow.

"It won't nauseate me," he said. "But it's up to Marisa." He gave her a crooked smile. "I'm totally out of my depth here. I know nothing about baby showers, and I just spent eighteen months in a country very different from this. Help me out here."

"You can come," Marisa said impulsively. "And you don't have to bring anything."

All of a sudden his eyes widened. "I picked up dessert at the bakery, and it's out in my car freezing." Without another word, he jumped up. An instant later they heard the door slam behind him.

Marisa and Julie shared a look. "I think he's okay," Julie said finally. "Sorry if I upset you."

"I think he's okay, too," Marisa agreed. "But he's a box full of secrets." She didn't want to admit how much that disturbed her.

"Just like another man we both knew and loved. Say, Marisa?"

"Yeah?"

"If you ever fall in love again, find someone uncomplicated. I know a teacher or two. You know, someone without secrets?"

Another laugh escaped Marisa as they heard Ryker come back in. "Yeah," she agreed. But she doubted that would ever happen. Losing one love had been enough for her lifetime.

And while Ryker was an attractive, sexy man, her response to that had been muted. She hoped it stayed that way.

Ryker left early, after dinner and a piece of the cake he had brought, and after insisting on doing the dishes. He was a man who was used to taking care of himself under far worse conditions. Washing dishes with running water felt like a luxury, although looking around the kitchen and thinking of the baby to come, he wondered if they could install a dishwasher in there. There seemed to be room.

But first the basement steps, he decided. Marisa hadn't refused his offer, so he supposed he ought to hit the lumberyard in the morning and buy what he'd need, as well as the angle brackets to attach to the crib. At least then he'd feel like he'd done more for John's wife than freshen her grief.

Marisa was a pretty armful. He could understand what John had seen in her, despite the grief that weighed her down now. If anything, pregnancy had made her blossom, although maybe the pictures John had shown him once hadn't done her justice.

And that Julie! The woman was something else, and he suspected that under better circumstances Marisa could be every bit as pointed and outspoken. Julie was protecting her friend from the possible threat he posed, and he approved of that, even though it had annoyed him a bit.

He was, after all, a stranger to them both, and John certainly hadn't been mistaken when he felt Marisa was safe here in the cradle of people who knew her. A very different life from his own, and he couldn't quite smother a flicker of envy.

It wasn't that he hadn't had decent friends over the years, John among them. But forged in the heat of a mission, they tended to be intense and brief. If you worked with the same guys repeatedly, as he had with John a number of times, something more enduring resulted. But with too many, the friendships had evaporated, either through death or dispersal.

Secrets weighted his soul the way grief weighted Marisa's. He'd never been a Ranger with John, although he let Marisa believe it. No, he'd always been an operative on the outside, working for the agency after his initial special ops training with the military. She, of course, had no idea what kind of missions John and his fellow soldiers had been sent on, dangerous missions behind the lines, in disguise, spying, gathering intelligence, always risking execution if they were discovered.

And deep in his heart he suspected John had been executed.

Marisa didn't need to know that, and without proof he was forced to doubt it himself. But she was right: A street mugging? He didn't believe it, and his web of contacts within the agency had quivered a little, letting him know that secrets were running around again, secrets about John's death.

He'd lived his whole life with secrecy, but lately he was coming to hate it. Having met Marisa, he hated it even more. He understood that the truth would probably serve no one in this case, but he was still distressed to know that Marisa didn't believe the cover story she'd been given. What would that do to her over time? Kill her ability to trust and believe?

He'd pretty much left his own behind.

He took a long run in the cold night air along the quiet streets of Conard City. The elements never bothered him, and he paid them only as much mind as he needed to for safety. A ski mask protected his nose, gloves protected his fingers and the rest of him stayed plenty warm from running.

He ran into the truck stop across from the motel just long enough to buy a couple of strong coffees, then headed back to his room. Not the Ritz, but he'd never stayed anywhere fancy. He was used to far worse and had learned to bed down just about anywhere he felt safe.

It was not a life he wanted to drag a woman into, even at long distance. John had managed it, but if Ryker had needed a reminder, Marisa had provided it. Some guys didn't worry about such things. They felt they could balance the two ends of the spectrum, but finally it came down to fairness, at least to his way of thinking. John might have loved Marisa completely, but as he'd thought before, there was something John had loved more than her.

As crazy as it might sound, John had been cheating on his wife with his job. Ryker preferred to just let it be known up front: he had one love and one love only.

He downed one of the coffees, took a hot shower, then flopped on the bed in a fresh set of sweats and stared at the ceiling while drinking his second coffee.

He might be used to being alone, but solitude wasn't always a good thing. He had no mission right now, other than to do whatever little things he could for Marisa, and more time on his hands than he wanted. Whenever he came home from an extended assignment, they gave him time to repatriate.

Funny word, but he understood it. Adapting to a foreign culture was somehow easier than coming home. Call it a mental health break or whatever, but they were giving him time to remember that he was all-American, apple pie, football-loving and all the rest of it. Making sure he had come fully home.

Regardless, time and guilt hung heavily on his hands. Something else, too, was creeping into his thoughts: awareness of Marisa as a woman. Neither of them needed that, and she sure as hell wouldn't want it.

But she was attractive as hell, even in her gravid state. Being around her was wakening the man in him in a totally unwelcome way. Man! He sat up and tried to shake it off.

Of all the unwelcome things he could feel. She was still deep in grief, pregnant with her dead husband's child, and he'd helped lead John to his death by getting him the damn job. It was a wonder she hadn't sent him on his way for that sin alone.

He took another swig of cooling coffee and reached for the self-control that locked away everything else inside him when he was on a mission. But that wasn't working now for some reason. He was drawn to Marisa, like it or not, and his mental shovel couldn't seem to bury it.

Maybe his bosses were right. Maybe they'd sensed something in him that had made them put him on enforced inactivity for longer than usual. Maybe John's death had hit him harder than he thought.

Death was his constant companion. He'd lost buddies before. Why should John be different? But somehow, in some deep way, he was. He had been, even before Ryker had decided to use this enforced break to keep his promise about Marisa. Why?

He racked his brains, trying to get at it. Compartmentalizing wasn't working. Nothing was working. John's death had struck him hard, harder than others. Maybe he felt personally responsible? But that was ridiculous. Men who took these jobs took them willingly. Nobody lied about the risks, ever. They might lie and conceal everything else, but not the risks. Once you were in the field, it was a very bad time to discover you couldn't handle the danger. And John had had plenty of previous experience. Some of the missions that Marisa would never know about had been CIA ones that used the Rangers, and John had known it.

He rubbed his hand over his face, feeling a day's stubble. Weird to be clean-shaven again. He still wasn't used to it. He wondered if he could go for that two-day's growth look that seemed so popular now.

He wondered if Marisa would like it.

Which brought him back to the guilt trip. He flopped back on the bed, telling himself not to be an idiot. Maybe he should just take care of those stairs, so she didn't hurt herself and the baby, and then clear out. It'd be safer.

But safer for whom? Himself? Marisa was so lost in grief and pregnancy that he was probably peripheral to her awareness of anything. So what if he wanted her? He could be certain she wouldn't feel the same about him.

Atonement, he reminded himself. Penance. Maybe hanging around and enduring his burgeoning desire for her was just part of the price he needed to pay. He'd already reopened her wounds. Who cared how uncomfortable this might be for him?

He'd withstood more in his life. Far worse than a little self-denial when it came to sex. Although sex was one place he hadn't practiced a whole lot of self-denial, except when on a mission.

Love, he realized, was the one thing he'd never allowed to blossom in his heart. He preferred it that way. He'd leave no one behind to grieve him. If he needed proof that he was being wise, there was a woman right across town.

A woman expecting a baby who'd never know its daddy. He never wanted to be responsible for that.

But in a different way, he was accepting responsibility for it. It hadn't been his choice, but it was still his responsibility. He owed that woman and child something. Hell, the whole damn agency did, but the most they ever managed was a letter and a star, and Marisa would never get those. If they had intended to tell her, she'd already know.

The secrets must be kept.

And suddenly, he hated them with every bit of passion he owned.

"Well, he was certainly interesting," Julie remarked later as she and Marisa curled up in the living room with some hot chocolate. "Did you see that flash of anger?"

"Yeah."

"All I did was ask him what took him so long to get here. You want my guess?"

"About why?"

Julie nodded. "I wish I had some marshmallows for this cocoa. My students have ruined me. I used to hate them. Anyway, he got mad because he felt bad about taking so long to get here. You must have noticed. Men get mad because it's easier for them than dealing with other emotional stuff."

Marisa gave a little laugh. "Sometimes, anyway."

"Well, that's my theory, and I'm sticking to it. They can't cry, so they throw things or punch something. They could learn from us. Anyway, he's an intriguing character. Attractive, too. He fluttered my little heart."

Now Marisa *did* laugh. "I thought you were recommending men without secrets. Like a teacher."

"Oh, definitely. If you want stability, avoid the bad boys." Then she caught herself and frowned. "Sorry, I wasn't including Johnny in that."

Marisa glanced down, eyeing her stomach, watching a small ripple pass across it. Her baby. Her touchstone. "Why not?" she asked finally. "Johnny was a bad boy. He liked danger. But he wasn't bad with me, or at home."

"Nope. Definitely not. He definitely worshipped you."

But not enough to give up the danger. The thought slammed into Marisa's mind, and a tiny gasp escaped her. No, she didn't want to think that way. Not about Johnny.

"Are you okay?" Julie asked swiftly.

"Just a little foot poking a rib. I'm fine." And now she was lying to her best friend, keeping her secrets. But she sure as heck didn't want to get into this with Julie. Not ever. In fact, she didn't even want to think it.

But the thought stayed in the back of her mind, refusing to go away.

"So," Julie went on, "are you going to let him work on the basement steps? He seems to want to."

"I think so," Marisa answered slowly. "They've been worrying me more and more often. Especially as ungainly as I am right now. One slip could be catastrophic." She paused. "Funny how things change. When I first married Johnny, I charged up and down those steps without a thought. But over the last few months—well, I guess I no longer feel indestructible or immortal."

"Actually," Julie said gently, "when you married Johnny a fall might have meant a broken bone. A fall when you're pregnant is a whole different thing."

"It feels like it."

"It's curious, though," Julie mused. "Ryker doesn't hang for long, does he? He came over, then vanished as soon as he'd finished cleaning up."

"He keeps saying he doesn't want to impose too much." She sighed and sipped cocoa. "Frankly, I don't think he's comfortable. When he walks in here, I get the sense that he feels like he's walking into an alien world."

"Probably is. Which I guess makes him sad in a way. Where the hell does a man like that belong?"

For once Marisa had no answer, because she had begun to wonder if Johnny had really felt he belonged with her. Oh, he'd loved her; he'd always come home to her. But belonging? Maybe it was different for him. He wasn't just coming back to her, but to the town he grew up in. Ryker didn't have that, not here. Maybe not anywhere.

Julie was right. That made him sad, no matter how strong, dangerous or driven he might be.

Chapter Four

This time Ryker called before he showed up. Marisa appreciated the gesture but was a little surprised by her reaction. Now that her first shock and discomfort had passed, she was looking forward to seeing him again.

A major change of pace, she assured herself. That was all it was. At this point she still distrusted him. Oh, she didn't fear he might hurt her or threaten her in any real way, but as she had phrased it to Julie, he was another box of secrets. If she hadn't known Johnny for so many years, she might not have been able to trust him enough to marry.

Because when you felt that there were large parts of a person you could never know, how did you offer them trust?

Not that that was an issue here. He'd stay for a little while, then go back to his secret world, and her life would resume.

Sometimes bitterness overtook her, and she wondered what life, what future, but the baby never missed an opportunity to remind her. Little Jonni, as she had started to think of the child, *was* her future, and all that mattered right now. The important thing was taking care of Johnny's final gift to her. Raising a daughter he would have been proud of. But sometimes she wondered if things might have been different if she'd been able to tell him she was expecting.

What would have been different? Would he have quit his job and settled into some boring path doing something he didn't love because he had a responsibility?

She wasn't sure that would have happened or worked out if it had. She'd bravely told Ryker that loving someone meant loving them just as they were, not trying to change them. She had done that with Johnny, so why even harbor any too-late hope that her pregnancy would have changed a thing?

Life had gutted her, and sometimes she grew angry. Extremely angry—a state that hadn't been familiar to her before. Sometimes she wanted to smash something. Throw something. Get even somehow. But none of that would have helped, and she knew it. Sometimes she wondered why life was so unfair, but even in the depths of misery she could look around and see that life was unfair to everyone. Fairness didn't even enter into it.

Since Ryker was coming and seemed to enjoy coffee, she made a fresh pot. Back in the early days of her pregnancy, when her doctor had limited her to two cups a day, she thought she was going be miserable forever. Now here she was six months later, and her two cups seemed more than ample.

Until right now. The brewing coffee smelled so good, she decided she might indulge. At this point, the restriction had been removed, but she had lost her old urge to drink the brew all day long. Right now, however, the aroma made her mouth water.

But as she waited for Ryker, some old, nearly forgotten instincts began to arise. She ought to be able to offer him something to eat. God, she hadn't done that even for her friends since word of Johnny's death. Not even now. Instead, Julie came over and cooked a meal for her, or her other friends dropped by with some tidbit and conversation. She'd become an ungracious mole.

It was a wonder she still had any friends, given how self-absorbed she'd become. She didn't laugh much, didn't say much and couldn't even welcome a guest with a cookie. She took, but she didn't give.

A new kind of guilt speared her, one she hadn't had room for since the funeral. Time, she guessed, to start dusting off her social skills again. Time to make an effort to participate, at least a little. The shower on Friday would be a good start. She hadn't wanted it, but she was getting it, and the girls were going to do it right here in her cave. She wouldn't even have to set foot out into the icy night; the party would come to her.

She made up her mind right then that she was going to enjoy it. Failing that, she'd make every effort to appear to be enjoying it. God, their patience with her was amazing, because being around her had to have been a serious downer all these months.

The doorbell rang, and she went to let Ryker in. Evidently the winter cold had returned in force. He stomped his feet as if to get blood flowing to them again, and pulled off his ski mask to give her a smile. "I've been to cold places before, but this one is heading to the top of my list."

"I haven't been paying attention." Sadly true.

"Take my word for it. It's beginning to feel like Antarctica."

She had started toward the kitchen but swung around instantly. "Was that hyperbole, or have you been there?"

She saw him hesitate. More secrets. Smothering a sigh, she started for the kitchen again. "I made a fresh pot of coffee for you. How are you managing at the motel?"

"The motel's fine. So is the truck stop diner."

"Try the City Diner sometime. Ask for it as Maude's diner, which is what everyone calls it. The service may be less friendly, but the food is fabulous."

"I'll remember that." As she entered the kitchen, with him following, he added, "Yes, I've been to Antarctica."

She froze, then turned to face him. He was shucking his jacket, hanging it over the back of one of the kitchen chairs. For an instant, just an instant, she thought that he looked like a hunk in flannel and jeans. She pulled herself back quickly, returning to curiosity. "For real? Are you allowed to tell me that?"

"I just did. Training exercise years ago."

"Wow," she said slowly. Not that she believed that was the whole story, but she decided to accept it. "I used to want to go there."

"What in the world for?" He sounded astonished.

A half smile tipped up one corner of her mouth. "I hear there are more shades of blue in the ice than we can imagine. And penguins. But I was thinking of a cruise."

"Ah." His smile returned. "Well, there *are* more shades of blue than you can imagine, if you have time to look at them. The penguins are smaller than you'd think, the seals more dangerous and the terrain and weather totally unforgiving. Which probably explains why no one except crazy scientists and crazy military people try to hang out there for long."

To her surprise, he drew a small laugh from her. Now, that wasn't so hard, was it? As she poured two mugs of coffee she said, "So, have you been on every continent?"

Again he didn't answer immediately. When she sat at the table, he sat, too. "No," he said finally. "And to answer the question you haven't asked, neither had John. And no, he didn't go to Antarctica as far as I know."

"That probably explains why he didn't quash my dream of taking that cruise someday." She stared into her coffee for a few seconds, thinking that it might be wise to back off this. This man was no more free to talk than Johnny had been. "So, what brought you today?"

"Well, I wanted a good look at those stairs to see what I'll need and figure out how to make them safer without taking over your entire basement. Measurements, mostly. Do you mind?"

She felt a flicker of warmth toward him, although she wasn't sure it was wise. "I really appreciate this. I'll pay for the materials."

He shook his head. "Call it my shower gift. It will probably take me a few days, though. Can you handle it?"

She decided she could. Internally, she'd made some kind of shift, she realized. She would never fully trust this man. She would always suspect he knew more about what had happened to Johnny than he would say, but she appreciated his willingness to deal with a problem for her.

"Are you a carpenter?" she asked.

"It used to be one of my hobbies. I can do stairs. Don't ask me to do any cabinetmaking. I don't have that level of skill."

"When did you learn?"

"My dad and I used to spend a lot of time in his shop. It was his hobby, too."

At last, something truly personal. That seemed important. She wondered where else she could safely wander. Then, an unexpected wave of resistance hit her. "I can hire someone to do it."

"All right." He sipped coffee before putting his mug down. "But you're not going to get rid of me that easily."

"Is that a threat?" Her heart slammed as she wondered if she had totally misjudged him.

"No, not at all." He shook his head. "I don't expect my feelings to matter to you, Marisa. Why should they? But understand this. I promised something to Johnny. You're going to find me as tough to get rid of as gum on the sole of your shoe."

"But why?" she demanded again. "Just tell me why, and don't tell me about promises. Just coming here fulfilled your promise. If I want you to go…"

"It's not just about promises. It's about debts. Guilt. Whatever you want to call it. I should never have gotten John that job. Never. I have to live with that." He sat there pinning her with his hard, dark gaze. "We all have our griefs and guilts, Marisa. All of us."

The raw honesty of that gripped her hard. Her lungs felt squeezed. "I don't want to be anyone's penance!"

"You're not my penance, believe me. You couldn't be if you tried. These are things I need to deal with myself. In the process, if I can help you out a little bit, it would be nice."

Understanding shook her. She wrapped her arms around herself. She could barely whisper. "You feel like you killed Johnny."

His face darkened until it looked like a winter sky, threatening, harsh.

"Did you?" she asked with the last bit of breath she could summon.

"I wasn't lying when I said I was in a different country." Without another word, he rose and left the kitchen. She half expected him to leave the house until she saw that his jacket was still there. She sucked air and rocked a bit, dealing with a blow she couldn't quite explain to herself. He felt responsible for Johnny's death, but in a way that went far past simply getting him a job. But why? What the hell was involved in that job? Translating shouldn't have been a deadly occupation.

Something was being withheld. The feeling that had overwhelmed her from the start battered at her again. She didn't know, she might never know, what had really happened, what Johnny had really been doing.

She listened to Ryker pace, felt her baby's stirrings as if they came from another world, and wondered how she was ever going to deal with any of this.

But oddly, as complicating as Ryker's presence was, even though she couldn't decide if she loathed him, and certainly knew that she didn't trust him, she felt a burgeoning seed of sympathy for him. She'd been so lost in her misery that she had forgotten that others had lost someone, too. That Ryker had not only lost a friend, but even felt responsible for it. The responsibility wasn't his. Even she knew that. The responsibility lay with Johnny's choices and whoever had attacked him. Ryker shouldn't have to shoulder that on top of anything else.

She had to live with loss and endless questions, but at least she didn't feel responsible. She couldn't imagine the weight of responsibility being added to all this hell.

For the first time since she got the news, she honestly thought about what someone else might be feeling. Actually cared that someone else was hurting, too. God, how utterly selfish she had become.

Standing back, for just a few seconds, she looked at herself and didn't like what she saw. Yes, grief was consuming, but it needn't rule out every other human feeling on the planet. In fact, she thought she might have been incredibly self-indulgent. Other people had to pick up the pieces after a death. They couldn't just withdraw into a private cocoon of hell, even if they wanted to. They had jobs and others they couldn't afford to forget.

"I'm weak," she announced.

Ryker's pacing in the foyer stopped. A moment later he appeared in the doorway. "You said something?"

"I'm just thinking about how weak I am." Might as well be truthful about something, and a near stranger seemed like a safer ear than even Julie right now.

"You're not weak," he said quietly.

"I disagree. I dropped out of everything. I put everything else on hold so I could curl up in a ball and feel sorry for myself."

"Grieving is not self-pity."

"Depends on how you do it, don't you think?" For the second time that morning, she felt scalded by understanding. Then she remembered something else. "You didn't kill Johnny. If there was one thing I learned as his wife, it's that he made his own decisions. If you hadn't found him that job, he'd have found another. It's how he was. How *you* are. You, of all people, should understand that."

Ryker visibly hesitated, shifting back and forth on his feet, as if he wasn't quite sure how to respond. She waved a hand. "You don't have to answer me," she told him. "Secrets. I get that part very clearly."

Slowly he came back to the table, as if he were dragging something heavy. He poured them both fresh coffee, then sat again. "Can we talk about John?"

She drew a long breath. "I guess we need to. He's here right now, right between us, still full of secrets I'll never know. Things I'll never understand. So go for it."

"I don't want to rip you up."

She swallowed hard. "I don't think anything can rip me up more than I already have been."

He nodded slowly. "Over the years John and I worked on a number of missions together. Not every one, but enough. The thing about me, about people like me, is that after a while you start to know exactly what you're capable of. Good and bad. What you can endure."

She nodded slowly. She guessed she could understand that.

"It doesn't usually take long for the brass to come off."

"Meaning?"

"You get to the point where you know you have nothing to prove to anyone, not to yourself, not to others. You've proven it already. So you kind of quiet down. That's what I meant about the brass going away."

"Okay." She sipped coffee, trying to wet a mouth that was turning dry. Somehow she knew she wasn't going to like this.

"John was different. I should have faced that difference more squarely. More honestly."

"How so?" She closed her eyes.

"He never stopped feeling he had something to prove. To whom or what I don't know. He rode himself hard. And—I'm sorry, Marisa—I wouldn't have taken that last post he took. If I had known, I'd have done my level best to talk him out of it. But he had something to prove. I knew that, and I should never have gotten him the job."

His words dropped into her heart like heavy stones of ice. She knew he was right but didn't know how to explain how she knew. John had always been involved in some kind of private competition. She'd always assumed it was with himself. "You're right about him," she admitted hoarsely. "I saw it sometimes."

"So that's where I failed you both. I knew he had a dangerous attitude, but I didn't act on that knowledge because I also knew he wasn't stupid. But more than once I had to remind him we were flesh and blood, not superheroes."

"Really?" Surprise opened her eyes. Amazingly, she could almost hear the conversation in her head. "I can believe that," she admitted. "Oh, I can believe that."

"Anyway, I'm not saying he did something stupid that got him killed. I know what you know. But I kind of feel like I should have guessed this might…happen."

The words emerged stiffly from her mouth. "You weren't his caretaker."

"No, but I evidently wasn't a very good friend, either."

Irritation sparked in her. "Do you really think he'd have listened to you? I know what he was like when he decided to do something. Wild horses couldn't stop him.

And if he felt he had something to prove, then that last job may have attracted him for that very reason."

His face softened a shade. "You're being very kind to me."

"No," she said, her tone sharpening. "I'm being brutally honest here. Maybe it's time I was. I loved him. I loved him with my whole being. But do you think he ever thought of that when he went away? When he made his decisions? No. I know he didn't. He always promised to come home, and I think he believed he always would. Maybe that's a dangerous way to live. But he sure didn't wonder about leaving me as a widow, or about the possibility of a child. I know because he *never once mentioned it to me.* I'm surprised he even thought about it enough to ask you to check on me."

"Marisa…"

"No." She silenced him. "He was a good man. He was always good to me. But there was a part of Johnny no one could ever tame. And I knew it, too."

Ryker closed his hands around his mug and looked down into it. "Maybe," he said finally. "But don't take it on yourself."

"I could no more take it on myself than I could control a wild mustang. He was who he was. We all are."

She put her hand to her forehead, then started to rise. "I need ice water. Enough coffee."

"Let me get it."

She let him do it because he seemed to need to do something, but as she watched him pull out the glass and deal with the ice dispenser on her fridge, she realized that she needed to do something, too. She was half ready to crawl out of her skin.

He placed a tall glass of ice water in front of her, and

she downed half of it immediately. Coffee, she had discovered, only made her thirstier.

He sat again, pushing the chair back and crossing his legs, one ankle on his knee. Leaning back, he cradled his coffee. "I didn't want to bash John. Don't take it that way. I wasn't saying he was reckless."

"Not exactly," she qualified. But in the deepest recesses of her being, she knew Johnny *had* been reckless. Not stupidly so, but she had taken some motorcycle rides with him in the mountains that had left her scared to death. He loved the adrenaline rush and kept on doing it even after she refused to go with him again. No sedate weekend drives for him. Nothing sedate about Johnny.

She looked at Ryker, who was studying the mug in his hands, and wondered how much like Johnny he was. He kept secrets, obviously, but he'd said he wouldn't have taken that last assignment that Johnny took. She desperately wanted to know why. But she knew the wall would slam in place again. Still, she had to ask.

"Ryker?"

"Yeah?"

"Why wouldn't you have taken that assignment?"

He glanced at her, those dark eyes drawing her in for just a moment before he returned his gaze to his mug. "Some situations," he said slowly, "are inherently unstable. Even a local lives in constant danger. So the key is to evaluate the situation. How much can I do? How helpful will I be? Or will I just be putting my head in a noose for no good reason? John and I had slightly different standards, I guess. If some good can be served, I'll go. If I judge that it can't…well, I've turned down a few postings. Not many, but a few."

"So you would have judged this one to be pointless?"

"Maybe not," he said quietly. "It's easy to judge in retrospect. John must have felt he could accomplish something while he was there. I shouldn't second-guess him now."

She reached out desperately for just another kernel. "But how much can a translator do?"

"Negotiate." One word, edged with warnings not to pursue it.

Unstable situation. Negotiation. She guessed he didn't mean the kind of negotiations she saw on TV with conference tables surrounded by serious men and women in business suits. She could imagine another kind, though, a much more dangerous kind. She didn't want to go there, but she suspected her late husband had done exactly that. And Ryker had just told her more than she had believed she could possibly learn. "Thank you," she said.

"Don't thank me. I'm not even sure I'm right. Like I said, I heard the same thing they told you. And that could be the truth, Marisa. I'm not saying it isn't. It could have been a random street attack, nothing to do with his job at all. Maybe someone thought he had money."

But she didn't believe it, and she suspected he didn't, either. He was as much in the dark as she was, and given that those walls of secrets that kept her out also kept him on the inside, it probably bothered him even more than it bothered her.

She drew a long breath, finally accepting that she would never know exactly what had happened. It was even possible that no one knew any more than they'd told her. Much as she hated the idea, it was possible, and she was going to have to live with it.

Studying Ryker, surprised by how much he had found a way to share with her, she noticed again how attractive he was. She'd felt the instant of recognition on their first meeting, but with him sitting there looking so relaxed, she let herself absorb it, this time without guilt. Maybe it was a good sign that she even noticed.

But he was so different from Johnny in appearance. Johnny had had a fresh-faced look to him, even when he came home after a long stint overseas. All-American guy looks. Ryker had a totally different impact. His black hair and eyes looked almost exotic, as if he had some Native American in him, and his skin was a few shades darker. His face had been chiseled into harsh lines, and today he apparently hadn't shaved, because dark beard growth shadowed his chin and cheeks. He was larger than Johnny, a few inches taller and a bit broader. Johnny had been solidly built, but this guy gave new meaning to the words. He might have been carved from granite. Appealing in a very different way.

But this was a path she didn't want to wander. It felt somehow like cheating on Johnny, although cheating on him was at least six months in her past. Not possible anymore, but a pang of guilt struck her again, anyway. Noticing another man with Johnny's baby in her belly. Betrayal.

"So," she asked, "do you prefer to be called R.T. or Ryker?"

He lifted his head, her words drawing a smile from him. "Ryker. It reminds me I'm home."

"It's an unusual name."

"Dutch. My mother's family had a few Rykers in the past. She dusted it off for me."

Marisa gave a little laugh. "Dusted it off?"

"Well, I think it skipped a few generations. My sister lucked out with Lila." Leaning forward, he put his cup on the table. "I need to go do my inspection and measuring. It looked like the tool shop downstairs was pretty well equipped. Mind if I explore it?"

"Help yourself." About the only things she was familiar with down there were the water heater, the heater, the humidifier and the washer and dryer. Other than to grab a wrench or a screwdriver from time to time, she really had no idea what wonders might be in the workshop area.

She needed to put her feet up for a while. She could feel her shoes growing tighter, so it was a relief when Ryker smiled, nodded and left the kitchen. Then, with another glass of water, she went into the living room where she could put her feet up on a hassock. Amazingly, it wasn't long before she fell asleep.

Ryker found some good work lights in the basement and positioned them so he could see the stairway clearly. He had plenty to think about as he used various measuring tools and a pencil and pad for note-taking.

He wondered if he'd spoken too harshly about John. The man had been a good friend for many years, but that didn't mean he couldn't see him clearly. John had not only kept his brass, but he'd remained unusually gung ho. His edge had grown harder with time, but it had never seemed to temper the way it did for most of them. If John had been brash when he'd come out of his Rangers training, he'd been just as brash the last time Ryker had seen him, nearly two years ago.

Turning down assignments wasn't something anyone did often, but they were allowed to. Not even the CIA wanted to send someone into a situation they didn't think they could survive. It wasn't like being in the army. You didn't have to salute sharply, then march up the hill into a hail of certain gunfire.

But given the country John had been sent to, Ryker was fairly certain he would have turned it down himself, maybe only the third time in his long career. It wasn't a job for cowards, but it was also a job that required a lot of smarts and street savvy. Clearly John had viewed his last assignment differently, but John had been a born risk-taker. They all were to a large extent, but John more than most.

He should have kept his mouth shut about that, even though Marisa had seemed to know the truth of it. The other stuff he'd told her, that was okay. No violation of operational secrecy. But being a translator? He had no difficulty imagining what Marisa had believed the job would be. It certainly wasn't standing as the lone man in a torn area of the world, probably trying to negotiate a prisoner release, or maybe a temporary cease-fire, or even to glean intelligence from dangerous sources. She had no idea of a world run by people who actually *liked* being at war, and to hell with everyone else. Nor would she even conceive that he might have been trying to infiltrate some subversive group.

But John had known. He had still walked in.

He admired John's guts. Someone had to do it. Once he'd been willing, but as he'd said, the years had taken some of the brass off him. These days it wasn't enough that a job needed doing. No, these days he calculated the likelihood of success versus failure…failure meaning death.

He wasn't afraid to die, but damned if he'd throw his life away in a pointless venture anymore. It all depended on what was on the line.

Maybe John's assignment had seemed important enough to take the risks. Maybe he'd judged that the value outweighed his own life. Well, of course he had. The question that would always hang over him was if John had misjudged. The world needed men like John, the ones who didn't count the cost.

But hell, when you had a wife... Ryker just shook his head. He and Marisa's husband were very different in one respect: Ryker had never let a woman get close enough to be singed by the fire. John had wanted it all.

And this was the end result. Ryker swore quietly under his breath, then switched off the lights and headed up the stairs to do some calculations at the kitchen table. He found Marisa dozing in the living room and couldn't quite suppress a smile. Remarkable woman. And in her late pregnancy, beautiful. An earth goddess, a vessel of life. Unlike him and John, who had been vessels of death all too often.

He'd never before noticed how sexy a pregnant woman could be, but this one had shown him. Lost as she was in the midst of her grief, something about her reached out to the man in him. He wanted her. Not wise. Her life had been shattered, and he didn't want to add to it.

Scolding himself, he went to the kitchen, filled a mug with the dregs from the coffeepot and sat down to figure out just how much lumber he was going to need. Minutes later, he was lost in sketching a diagram of the work ahead of him.

Marisa awoke to find the house empty, and relief flooded her along with a tide of shame. Thank God he wasn't here. She felt horrified by the vivid dream that had startled her into consciousness, a dream of making love with Ryker. How could she even…?

She guessed her somnolent libido was reawakening, but did it have to be Ryker? A real man who was in her life right now?

No gauze covered the memory of the dream. No symbolism had filled it, making it hard to be sure what she had dreamt. It had been as vivid, as detailed, as real as a pornographic film. She couldn't remember ever having a dream like that.

It had left her aching with desire. The longing throb between her thighs followed her into the real world, holding her frozen in her seat despite being able to see that Ryker's car was gone. Despite knowing she was alone and no one could possibly see the heat in her cheeks.

But the feeling…it shamed her, but she wanted to hang on to it. It had been so long since her body had cried out for a man's touches, but it was crying now. *Love me. Fill me. Take me.*

It pounded through her blood like a song that wouldn't quit. What the heck was happening to her? She didn't have feelings for Ryker. Sometimes she wished he'd never shown up. She even occasionally wished he'd just go away.

What had she been thinking to agree to allow him to fix the stairs? Now he'd be around longer. Now he'd even attend her baby shower, a man in place of her husband.

She didn't want to replace Johnny. Hell, she never wanted to walk that road again.

Ryker?

But her subconscious had launched it into her awareness, and no amount of mental shoveling could make it go away. Okay, so she'd had a dream. A delicious dream.

But just a dream and she didn't have to tell anyone, nor did she have to act on it.

Guilt grabbed her again, the feeling that she might betray Johnny. But even as it did, she heard Johnny's old familiar laugh in her head. *Just go for it.* How many times had he told her that? How many times had Johnny done exactly that? He believed in going for what you wanted. If he'd ever felt guilt about anything, she didn't know it.

Johnny-in-the-moment. Always in the here and now. Hell, he'd be egging her on, she thought grumpily. He often had.

The remembered dream clung and, with it, physical sensations almost as if Ryker really had touched her, and her cells remembered each caress. Finally, she glanced down at her ankles and saw the swelling had subsided. Time to get up, get some water and think about dinner.

When she meandered into the kitchen, she saw papers scattered on the table. Taking a look at them, she realized Ryker had been doing calculations and drawings for the staircase. As she scanned them, she decided he did seem to know what he was doing.

Good, because she'd be in a mess if she couldn't reach the basement. The forced air heat kicked on, stirring the air and, for just a moment, letting her feel a chill.

Dinner, she reminded herself. But for how many?

The question almost overwhelmed her. For the first time in ages, she needed to consider it, and she didn't even know if Ryker would be there. She could have laughed, had she felt more like it. But the dream haunted her, making laughter seem almost criminal.

Peering into her freezer, she wondered if she had enough of anything to make a meal for two. She didn't even know what Ryker liked or how much he ate. Johnny had always had a huge appetite, but considering how in shape he always was, and that he invariably came home from every mission looking as if he'd lost ten pounds or more, of course he'd been a heavy hitter. One of the hardest things she'd always had to deal with was making the mental shift from cooking for two to cooking for one. Although now she wondered how she could ever have thought that hard. Life had shown her just how sheltered she had been until recently.

Now her brain didn't seem to want to shift in another direction. She peered into her freezer, looking for something she had time to thaw that she might adequately turn into a meal for two. The pickings were slim, however, so she headed to the pantry. She always kept broth on hand, and it could readily be turned into a soup with some noodles and vegetables. At least if she ate alone tonight, the soup would still be good tomorrow.

Just as she was reaching for the carton of chicken broth, she heard the front door open and close. Ryker?

"Marisa?" she heard him call.

"In the kitchen."

She heard his steps cross the foyer and turned from the pantry in time to see him carry in a large paper bag. "I found Maude's," he said with a smile. "You were right about the service."

"Everyone's used to it."

"Anyway, I took a chance and brought something for us to eat. Interesting thing happened."

She realized she was devouring him with her eyes and fought to drag her gaze to the bag. "What?"

"The incredibly angry woman who runs the place asked if I was buying dinner for you, too. I said I was. She picked out your meal for tonight."

Despite everything, a laugh overtook Marisa, and she had to grab the back of a chair and hold her side. "Oh, that's Maude," she said breathlessly.

"So I gathered. I also gathered at least half the town knows I'm here to see you. Great intelligence network."

"Fiona," she answered.

"Fiona?"

"My next-door neighbor. I'm surprised she hasn't come over here to give you the third degree. Anyway, she was the first to see you, and the entire reason Julie came to check you out. If you want secrecy, you won't find it in this town."

He flashed a smile. "I'm already discovering the usefulness of that. I ordered supplies at the lumberyard, and they'll be delivered tomorrow. Two guys are going to help get them down your stairs, and I'm reliably informed by one of them—Hank, I think it was—"

"That'd be Kelly's husband. You'll meet him Friday night."

He absorbed that. "Okay, then. Anyway, he says more than one person has lately been worrying about you on those stairs, so it seems I'm going to have some help."

She gripped the chair with her other hand. "Heavens!"

He shrugged and started pulling foam containers and beverages out of the bag. "I think it's great. We'll make short work of it this way and cause you less commotion." He raised his gaze as he put the last beverage container on the table. "I can see why Johnny believed you were safe here. The gargoyle at the diner knew what you'd want to eat, and three guys at the lumberyard couldn't wait to help with your stairs. That's special."

She nodded, admitting it. People around here could be very special, yet she'd been avoiding them like the plague. What did that make her? "I never even mentioned the stairs," she said, lacking a more appropriate response.

"Well, according to Hank, his wife went down them once after…the funeral, to help you out with the wash, and she's been muttering ever since. He said, unfortunately, he couldn't afford to do it himself."

She shook her head. "Hank and Kelly have a lean budget."

"Well, I don't. I suspect from the way they were talking there was some discussion of trying to get a pool going to fund the supplies. So we'll start on Saturday."

"Wow," she whispered. She paused just long enough to get her glass of ice water, then slid into a chair at the table.

"Maude sent you hot cocoa," he said, pushing a foam cup her way. "Something about you being restricted on coffee?"

A surprised laugh escaped her. "You know, Johnny kept his secrets, but I guess I don't have any."

Ryker slid into a seat across from her. "I like it here," he announced. "I've seen other close-knit places like this all over the world, but I was always the outsider. You're fortunate to have these people."

She thought then about the amazing loneliness he must live with and felt a pang. Not knowing what she could say without offering offense in some way, she opened the foam container and found that Maude had sent her a Cobb salad loaded with turkey and conspicuously lacking bacon. She smiled as she looked at it. Caring even from Maude, who rarely showed any.

"I liked the guys I met," he remarked. "They all seem like good sorts."

A few minutes later, as they ate, he spoke again. "You've grown awfully quiet. Are you okay?"

"I'm fine. It's just that you reminded me of something I lost track of after Johnny. How good my friends are. How lucky I am to have them."

He swallowed another bite of his sandwich before replying. She watched him wash it down with his own drink, which appeared to be coffee. "You know," he said, "I can see why John could leave you behind, knowing you had these people around you. He relied on them. And I can also understand why you've lost sight of them since John died. Some things are so huge they don't leave room for much else."

"Grief," she replied, "is totally selfish, as I've just begun to realize."

"It's also overwhelming. Cut yourself some slack."

She raised her gaze to his face. "How much slack do you cut yourself?"

He didn't answer, which she decided meant he didn't cut himself much slack. He was here, wasn't he? Keeping a sort-of promise he'd made to Johnny back when. She hadn't exactly given him a gracious welcome, but he had told her that he was stuck to her like gum to the sole of a shoe—apparently until he decided he'd kept his word.

"So when's your due date?" he asked.

"Two and a half months, give or take."

"You don't look that far along…not that I'm a great judge."

"Well, I am. I expect I'll get really big soon. But not everyone does, I guess."

"Girl or boy?"

"Girl."

She caught sight of his smile. "It's been a long time

since anyone had to wonder. Must have been very different when you didn't know whether to get blue or pink."

She managed a laugh. "Like the baby would care."

He joined her laugh. "Probably not. But isn't that designed to avoid all those mistaken comments about the baby's sex?"

"Maybe. I don't know. What's the point of getting bothered by that? I can't imagine getting offended by a pronoun."

He laughed again. "You might feel differently after the hundredth time. But then I guess around here word will travel fast. Probably won't be a problem if you dress the girl in orange."

She smiled but then realized she was getting tired again. Having someone around so much had become taxing. And Ryker, though he didn't mean to be, was especially taxing. He was wakening feelings in her she didn't want and making her think about how she had changed in ways she didn't like.

As if he sensed her fatigue, he left as soon as he finished eating, promising to see her tomorrow night at the shower.

She was relieved that he was gone and strangely disappointed that he didn't intend to come back until the shower. She guessed the lumberyard would deliver without his supervision.

That was for the best, wasn't it? She didn't need to cultivate a relationship with him. He was part of Johnny's past, and she didn't want him to be part of her future.

At some deep level, she still felt distrusting. They'd get through the baby shower and then the stairs, and then she'd try to send him on his way.

Because she absolutely didn't like the painful awakening he stirred inside her, and she didn't want to emerge from her cave just yet. Her desire for him felt like a betrayal, and he wasn't the staying kind, anyway.

So even if she hadn't felt that he was still guarding secrets and keeping her in the dark, she would have still wanted him gone.

Ryker Tremaine was trouble. He had to leave.

Chapter Five

Ryker attended the baby shower but left as early as he could. All the oohing and aahing over tiny clothes in every color of the rainbow and over a ton of other baby supplies didn't interest him.

Well, it didn't exactly repel him, but it reminded him of how empty his own life had been except for work. He was nearly forty and had just discovered the whole concept of baby showers. There was something wrong with the way he lived his life.

By choice, he reminded himself as his feet pounded cold pavement. In his motel room, he did endless sit-ups and push-ups and wished for a gym.

Then they went to work on the staircase. He liked the three other guys well enough, Hank and his cohorts, but they were as far from his world as it was possible to be. He listened to their conversation, occasionally managed to join in some of the joking, but mostly just kept his mouth shut. They had the new stairs done by Sunday night and watched Marisa try them out. She smiled hugely and thanked them repeatedly…and once again he exited as quickly as he decently could.

One of his greatest survival mechanisms was being able to read people, and he was reading Marisa. She was uncomfortable around him. She didn't trust him much, justifiably so. And judging by the way her gaze skated past him so often, she didn't really want him there.

So he stayed away. He should have left town, but something made him hang around, anyway. He'd made a promise of sorts, and somehow sticking his nose in the front door and helping build some stairs didn't leave him feeling as if he was done with it.

But what could Marisa need him for? She had an ample number of concerned friends. He was no one to her, except possibly the man who had gotten her husband into a deadly situation.

He sent out some feelers, trying to get more information about what had happened to John Hayes, wondering at himself even as he did so. Did he really need any more secrets to conceal from a grieving widow? But he still wanted to know, and he still didn't learn a thing. The cloak of secrecy that had been thrown over John's final activities was as impenetrable as steel.

That bothered him, too. He was beginning to see the organization he worked for in a new light, one shone on it by Marisa's loss. The agency was built on secrets, swamped in them, but for someone supposedly on the inside to be unable to learn even something small? Whatever they had asked of John, they didn't want anyone to know. The secrecy was so deep they didn't even have a decent cover story to share in-house. It was as if John had never existed, except for one anonymous black star on a wall.

Then, a few weeks later, while still wrestling with his own demons and trying to ignore the Christmas decorations that had popped up everywhere, he ran into Marisa and almost didn't recognize her. She was coming out of a doctor's office, and her belly had ballooned. Late pregnancy was truly on her. He wondered if she was nearing term, despite what she'd told him.

She saw him and froze mid-step.

"Hi," he said, slowing his jog and stopping. "How are you?"

"I'm fine," she said hesitantly. "I didn't know you were still in town."

He doubted that. "Well, I don't need to go back, and I kind of like the place."

"Like gum on my shoe," she remarked.

"Hey, I've been staying away. I know you don't like me being around."

A frown trembled around her mouth, though he could see she was making a valiant attempt to smile. "It's true," she admitted finally. "Go home, Ryker."

Wind cut through his jogging clothes, despite the jacket and gloves. "Where's that?" he asked rhetorically, starting to run in place.

"This is creepy. I feel stalked."

"I haven't bothered you anymore," he argued, keeping his tone level. "I got the message."

"And it's a free country," she said sharply.

"Last I heard. Look, I don't want to fight with you. I'm staying out of your way. Let's just leave it, okay?"

He started to pass her, but her voice stopped him.

"You don't have a home?"

He hesitated. "Depends on what you mean by that."

"Oh, for the love of…" She broke off. Then, almost a command, she said, "Follow me home."

"Why?"

"Because I want to talk."

"You've got plenty of friends."

She drew a breath. "But they're not you." Without another word, she walked around a car and climbed in behind the wheel.

"Should you be driving?" he called after her.

"Who else will do it for me?" She revved the engine and drove away, leaving him somewhere near hell's door as he wondered if he should follow her or ignore her. He certainly hadn't come here to make her life harder.

But his feet seemed to have a mind of their own and carried him toward Marisa's place. He guessed they were going to have it out. Maybe then he'd be free to leave.

She opened the door to him, and he stepped in from the cold. Odd how symbolic that suddenly seemed. "I made you coffee. I need to get my feet up."

"Something wrong?"

"Pregnancy. Nothing's wrong."

"You want coffee, too?"

"Sure, why not?"

Hardly inviting, but she'd seldom been inviting toward him. He was like a mess she didn't know how to clean up. He got it. He just wished he could explain what kept him stapled here when he was clearly so unwanted.

He brought coffee into the living room and found her in the rocker with her feet up on the hassock. "Badly swollen?" he asked, trying to be polite.

"It's becoming more common, but the doc isn't too

worried. Just spend a little less time on my feet and put them up when I can."

Well, that was more than she'd been sharing since their first meeting. Was that good or bad? "So, what's been keeping you on your feet?"

She surprised him then, laughing softly. "Nesting."

"Nesting?"

"I was warned this would happen toward the end of my term. Cleaning binge. Getting everything ready."

"The crib is sorted out?" He'd managed to put those brackets in for her in the midst of handling the staircase.

"Go look," she said, waving her hand.

So he did. The crib was at the foot of her bed, a mattress in place, the bedding all made up, pads around the entire thing for protection, he supposed. He had to do a lot of guessing when it came to babies. He'd learned some things after his sister was born, but a ten-year-old boy didn't pay attention to many of the details. A mobile hung from the ceiling, and he imagined one of her friends had done that for her. Soft cartoon characters hung from it. The top of her dresser looked ready to be a changing table.

He returned to the living room feeling odd in some way. Preparation for a new life. Never had he felt more out in the cold. He perched on the edge of the couch, alert, ready to leave as quickly as necessary. Hell, he lived most of his life that way.

"So you don't have a home?" she said.

"Not really. I'm gone too much."

She nodded. "Johnny was, too." Then she surprised him. "I've been rude to you."

"No—"

"Yes," she interrupted. "Rude. You were Johnny's

friend. Apparently, a good enough friend to come to the back of beyond to check on his wife. I've treated you exactly like that gum on my shoe."

"It's okay."

"No," she said hotly, "it's not okay. You were my husband's friend, one of the best he had, and I've treated you poorly. I didn't want you here."

There, she'd said it. He edged forward, ready to leave.

"But the thing is," she continued, "I didn't want you here for reasons that weren't fair to you."

He hesitated, wondering if he should speak at all.

"You reminded me, not just of Johnny, but of the person I used to be. I'd become something awful, and I had some time to think about it. *You* made me think about it. I'd become a hermit. I'm surprised all my friends didn't abandon me, and then you…you got me thinking about what I was doing. Grief *is* selfish, but it doesn't have to be this selfish. I didn't want you here because you made me see myself. It wasn't a pretty picture."

"But an understandable one," he said in what he hoped was a kind voice. It was a voice he didn't get to use often.

"Maybe or maybe not. The point is, I woke up to the fact that I was making things worse for everyone around me, and I wasn't dealing. Not really. I was hiding in my misery. Then it struck me that misery is, if not comfortable, at least a safe place to stay. It takes no risks."

He tried to sort thought all this, to understand what she was driving at, but he wasn't at all sure.

"Anyway, you made me uncomfortable, and a lot of it had to do with me. I have a right to grieve, but not to wallow in self-pity and to hurt my friends because it hurt me to see them."

He grasped that. "It hurts to see others happy when you're not."

"So what? They have a right to be happy, and I should be happy for them, not hating them for it. Loss comes to everyone, Ryker. I tried to remind myself that you'd lost Johnny, too, but...well, maybe that was the first thing that made me look harder at myself."

His chest tightened for her. God, all the things this woman had to deal with. He was amazed that she could even find concern for others with all that had happened. "Don't be hard on yourself."

"Why not? I'm not the only widow in the world. It happens to thousands every single day. I just let it suck me down like quicksand. I shut out everything and everyone. I'm not very proud of it. Anyway, get your stuff from the motel. You can stay in one of the spare rooms."

He felt he'd just been gut-punched. Was she having some kind of break? A moment of insanity? Stay in this house with a woman he'd bed in an instant if she crooked a finger his way?

"No, really..."

"I'm serious. You may not be a talker, but I'd like to know you better."

"Because of Johnny?" He was definitely wrestling with this.

"Not just that. For me, too. And anyway, I need someone around. You want to help, I need help. Right?"

"Yes," he answered promptly, although the request for help left him feeling a little deflated. For the last few weeks, despite all the time he'd spent trying to cut Marisa out of his thoughts, she'd simply taken up firmer residence there. He'd have liked it if she just wanted him around. Not that that was ever going to happen. Was he losing his mind? He usually met life with more clarity than this. "What kind of help?"

"A little of everything, but mainly I need someone around because the doctor told me he thinks I'm farther along than he originally thought. I may need someone to drive me to the hospital all of a sudden."

"Farther along?" Now he was in the weeds in a swamp he didn't begin to understand. Pregnancy had not been a part of his life. "How is that possible?"

"It's possible. Johnny was home for a little over two months. I could have been pregnant the first two months without even knowing it."

He sensed the details of that were something he should leave alone. "So is he sure?"

"Pretty much. He judges the baby to be over seven pounds right now. Either I'm going to have an elephant or I'm getting close to term. I'd rather not have an elephant."

That surprised a crack of laughter from him. "I read you."

She smiled faintly. "Given the range of time…well, we're just hoping that her lungs are fully developed when she arrives. That's why I don't want to be early. But if he's right…Jonni could be here in the next few weeks."

"I like the name," he offered.

"It seemed to have stuck without me even thinking about it. Not really. I didn't even indulge in looking up baby's names. So she's probably going to be Johnna, Jonni for short."

"Pretty. So this nesting thing? It's for real?" He was surprisingly curious about all this. Something totally new in his life, and he evidently needed it. Great big gaping holes in his experience stared him in the face. Sometimes he felt as if he'd become a one-dimensional man.

"My friends tell me it means I'm getting close, maybe in the last month. Connie loves to talk about moving a two-hundred-pound couch all by herself because she simply had to rearrange the living room. And I've certainly been on a cleaning binge. Even the insides of my kitchen cabinets are sparkling."

"I could have helped with that." Lame, but all he could think of when he was still trying to wend his way through this, trying to figure out what this woman was really saying.

"I'm sure. And if I get an urge to wash windows, I'll put you to work."

For the first time, he relaxed. Some kind of relationship was being laid out here, and so far he didn't have any problems with it. "Fair enough. I need the workout."

Was he really agreeing to move into this woman's house? He guessed he was, which was sure going to make life difficult.

Marisa sighed and put her cup aside. "I'm perfectly healthy, the baby is doing great, I just get tired more easily. Normal activities are all allowed."

Meaning? He didn't know if he should ask. But then a thought struck him, a thought so alien to him that he had to digest it before speaking. This woman had a big hole in her life, yes, but there was an even bigger hole. She didn't have a husband to share this experience with, to talk about her baby with, to discuss each development along the way. He might not know a lot about it, but he suspected pregnancy was a huge deal for a woman, and she ought to have someone to share it with. Marisa had been missing the most important part of that.

He asked carefully, "Do you talk to your friends about your pregnancy?"

"Sometimes. Well, rarely. It's not like it's a big thing for them the way it is for me. Besides, like I said, I've been hiding away. Staying inside myself."

"Well, I don't know squat about it," he said truthfully. Rising, he put his own cup down and crossed the room. He lifted her ankles from the hassock, feeling that simple touch like an electrical shock, and sat with her feet on his thighs. Gently he started rubbing her ankles. "I'd like to know," he said quietly. "Tell me about it."

The frozen way she looked at his hands, he expected her to tell him to keep his mitts to himself. But then she astonished him. With a smile, she said, "That feels so good."

"Then I'll keep it up." Carefully he removed her jogging shoes, leaving her socks in place, and began to rub her feet, as well. It felt like sparks were shooting from his hands, or from her feet to his hands. "So talk to me. Despite everything, you must have had some special moments after you learned you were expecting."

"I did." Utter relaxation appeared to pass through her, and she let her head fall back and her eyes close. "There was the first time I felt movement. It was…amazing. All of a sudden this baby was real, totally real to me. It changed everything."

"What did it feel like?"

"At first almost like small bubbles moving. Now it's stronger. I get definite pokes and kicks."

"Can you see them?"

"I sure can. Sometimes I think I can even make out a foot, just this tiny little wedge, but I'm not sure. As the doc said, the baby's inside a pillow which is inside another pillow."

"But you've seen an ultrasound?"

"This morning." Her eyes didn't open, but a smile came to her face. "She's so perfect."

"Did you get to keep a picture?"

"It's in my purse."

"I'd like to see it later."

Her eyes opened. "Ryker? Why are you doing this? You don't need to get involved with the baby."

He thought about that before answering. "I've led an active life, but there are lots of things I've missed. This is one of them. And besides, the baby is John's legacy."

"Legacy," she repeated the word. "I like that."

He rubbed her feet, extending her toes, massaging the muscles along her arches, then returning to her ankles, rubbing gently to move the fluid upward. "We're different in a very important way."

"What's that?"

"You create life. You bring something wonderful into the world."

She tilted her head. "And you don't?"

"I try to save lives, yeah. But it's not always possible."

Another sigh escaped her, and her eyes closed. "That's sad. And I could sleep."

"You just do that. While you nap, I'll get my belongings from the motel."

She nodded slightly, and he watched with a faint smile as she dozed off. Only when he was sure she slept did he stop massaging her.

She was giving him a totally different perspective on life, he thought as he grabbed his coat and headed out. That could be a good thing or a very bad thing.

One thing for sure. He was beginning to wonder how John could have ever left this woman's side.

After he'd filled his duffel and backpack, which pretty much contained his whole life except for some items in storage in Virginia, he headed for the diner. He was recognized when he entered and greeted by some of the folks having lunch there. While he didn't feel as if he were part of their community, he guessed they were letting him know that they'd decided he was okay.

Even irascible Maude gave him a nod and asked what he wanted. As soon as she heard he was buying for two, she asked if it was for Marisa. When he answered yes, Maude went to work making a meal.

"She swelling any?" Maude asked.

"Her ankles and feet."

"I'll leave off the salt, then. I swear that woman looks ready to pop any day."

Ryker didn't offer any gossip. Keeping secrets was nearly automatic.

"She needs someone looking after her now." Maude glared at him. "Any volunteers?"

He almost laughed at her pointedness. He'd known gunnery sergeants who didn't hold a candle to this woman. "Yes, ma'am. Me."

"About time," Maude grunted, then went back to work. Quite soon she had a paper bag full of foam containers and beverages. Ryker stepped out into the bracing cold and found himself face-to-face with a guy in a sheriff's uniform. One side of his face was burn-scarred, and his badge said "Dalton."

So this was the sheriff he'd heard about a couple of

times. "Put that food in the car," the man said. "Let it keep warm. I just want a word."

Ryker nodded, put the bag on the passenger seat, then faced the man. He wore a heavy shearling coat, but the badge and name tag were sill prominent, as were patches on the shoulder. He offered his hand.

"Gage Dalton, sheriff," he said. "And you're Ryker Tremaine."

"Yes."

"I got word you checked out of the motel. Leaving town?"

"Marisa Hayes asked me to stay with her."

Dalton nodded slowly. "I checked up on you. I still have some pretty good contacts from my days with the DEA."

Ryker tensed. What was this about?

"You have an amazingly bland background," Dalton remarked. "Which tells me a whole lot. The absence of information is often very informative."

Ryker waited, vigilant, for whatever was to come.

"Just be careful," Dalton said. "I don't think Marisa could handle another John, if you get my drift."

"Perfectly."

Dalton nodded and walked back toward his office up the street. Ryker stood there for a minute. The man was right. Marisa couldn't handle it again. But he already knew that. What struck him was the way this town kept trying to protect her. Even the damn sheriff.

He figured that living here could either make a person claustrophobic or very grateful. So far he didn't feel claustrophobic, but then he wasn't trying to put down roots here. Maybe folks were pretty much leaving him alone.

He took the warning in good part, even though he didn't need it. He knew he was poison. That was why he'd never stayed long enough to get attached. This was different, however. Between repatriation time after his last mission and having a whole lot of built-up vacation time, he could stay as long as he wanted.

But only if he didn't feel he was hurting anyone. Marisa had her doubts about him, justifiably so. He might want to take her to bed, maybe even indulge in a little fantasy about a life with her, but that was all it would ever be: fantasy.

Because Marisa carried a price tag. He'd have to give up his job to be what she needed, to spare her another loss. The thought was so impossible that he'd never considered it.

Not before Marisa, anyway.

Crap, he was a mess. He needed to square his head away, and he needed to do it soon.

When he got back to the house, he left his bags in the car and went inside with the food. She was gone from her rocker, evidently done with her nap.

"Marisa?"

"In the kitchen."

He walked through the door and froze. She was standing on the top of a three-step stool, reaching for something well above her head.

"My God, woman! What the hell…?"

"I wanted that casserole dish from up there," she said. "It didn't use to be so high."

He saw her teeter a bit. He moved in a flash, dropping the bag on the table as he passed it and catching her by the hips, steadying her. "Are you out of your mind?"

"Oh, hush, Ryker. I've done this a million times."

"Probably not with about twenty pounds hanging off your front affecting your balance. Down. Now. I'll get the damn dish."

"Sheesh," she said, but a little giggle escaped her. "I think the nesting hit again."

"I think you're out of your mind. Step down. Easy now. I've got you."

With each step down, her back brushed the front of his body, stoking fires he'd been trying to put out almost from the first instant he saw her. "You know," he muttered, "this sucks. And you shouldn't be allowed to be alone for even ten minutes if you're going to pull stunts like this."

"Maybe not," she said quietly, then astonished him by leaning back into him as her feet settled on the floor. His hands remained on her hips, and he stopped breathing as she covered them with her own.

What was the she up to?

"You have big hands," she remarked. "Strong." Her fingers curled briefly around his and squeezed. "Thanks. Forget the casserole. I have others."

"But you wanted this one enough to risk your neck."

"It was my grandmother's. I mainly wanted it down where I could see it. Pure decoration. Ryker? I think my back hurts a bit."

Well, he could sure understand why, given the way she had been reaching and that twist to look at him when he first arrived. "Where?" he asked.

"High up. Not low. Don't panic, it's not labor."

Panicking wasn't usually in his nature, although he supposed anything was possible. But he didn't want to let go of this moment of intimacy, however pointless and brief it was. He had begun to crave this woman, and a stupider thing he'd never done.

Slowly she released his hands. Taking it as a sign, he stepped back. He cleared his throat, feeling uncharacteristically awkward. "I brought food from the diner. A warning, though. Maude left the salt off yours."

She turned slowly, her cheeks flushed. "Nice of her."

He guided her to her chair and began pulling items out of the bag. His groin throbbed, and he hoped she couldn't see it. His jeans weren't that tight, he assured himself, and his black sweatshirt was extra long, providing a little more camouflage.

"Ryker?" She sounded breathless. Concerned, he looked up from the bag.

"What?"

"Am I awful?"

"Awful? What in the world would make you think that?"

"Because...because..." She put her face in her hands.

At once he squatted beside her, worried, touching her arm. "Marisa? What's wrong?"

"Nothing. It's just...I shouldn't be having these feelings."

"What feelings?" Suicidal thoughts? Urges to kill someone? Fear? The whole palette of emotions lay there waiting for her to choose one.

She kept her face covered. "I have dreams about you."

His entire body leaped. He had dreams about her, too, and not only when he was sleeping. "And?"

"I want you. Is that wrong? I mean...it hasn't been that long..."

Her words deprived him of breath. He could have lifted her right then and carried her to her bed. He'd have done so joyfully. But caution and maybe even some wisdom held him back.

"I want you, too," he said huskily.

She dropped her hands, her wondering eyes meeting his almost shyly. "Really? Looking like this?"

"You're beautiful looking just like that. But…"

"But?" She seized on the word, some of the wonder leaving her face.

"I don't want you to regret it. So how about we spend more time talking to each other? Give yourself some time to be sure. Hell, it probably wouldn't be safe, anyway."

"My doc says it would."

She'd asked her doctor? A thousand explosions went off in his head, leaving him almost blind. He cleared his throat. "Uh…I could take you right now. I want to. So, please, don't be embarrassed. I don't think you're awful. But…please…get to know me a bit better. I want to know you better. I want you to be sure."

"I feel guilty," she admitted. "It's been driving me nuts. Am I betraying Johnny?"

"I don't believe he'd think so. But that's a question only you can answer, and you need to do that for yourself. Then there's me."

"You?" She studied him.

"I don't exactly feel right about this. After what you've already been through, I shouldn't have to explain that. I'm another John, Marisa. Why in the world would you want to risk that again?" And now that he knew the real reason she'd been trying to avoid him, he felt like crap. He'd read her all right. She wanted him gone. But only because she wanted *him*, and it made her feel guilty. Could it get any messier?

She nodded slowly, looking down at where her fingertips pressed into the wooden table. "I don't know," she finally said quietly. "Not that it'd be a risk. You already said you don't commit."

At a rather advanced stage of life, he was discovering how fast feelings could grow. It was as if he'd let something off his internal leash, and now he hurt to hear himself described in his own terms. "Think about it," he said. "Just think about it. I'll be living here for a while, so you can find out if this is what you really want. In the meantime, let's chow down before the food gets cold."

He hated to remove his hand from her arm, to withdraw to a safer distance. Food held little appeal now, because he knew he didn't just need her to evaluate her feelings, but he needed to evaluate his whole damn life.

Later, after he'd cleaned up and put half her salad in the fridge for later, he retrieved her casserole dish for her. "It's pretty," he said. It was cobalt blue, with pink flowers and gold scrolling.

"I always thought so." Then she shook him to the core. "You know I've been avoiding you."

"I know. Same here. I could tell you didn't want me around, so I stayed away."

"But do you know why I felt that way?"

"Tell me." So it wasn't all about illicit feelings of desire. He didn't know whether to be relieved.

She hesitated while he set the casserole dish on the counter and put the stool away. "I didn't trust you. Too many secrets. And then I wanted you, and I felt guilty. Did I upset you by telling you that?"

He faced her squarely. "Truth is always welcome in my life." A rare commodity, if he were to be honest. "No, you didn't upset me. Why should you trust me? But you shouldn't feel guilty."

"But I hate that you know things about Johnny I can never know."

Ouch. His mind raced, seeking adequate words to give her. There were none. There would never be any. "I can't tell you," he said finally.

"I know. But why do I think there are things I wouldn't want to know even if you could?"

"Because you're probably right," he said brutally. "What we did…what we sometimes had to do…you don't need to know about it."

She nodded, drawing a shaky breath. "I suspected. I didn't want to think about it, but I suspected. Someone has to do the world's dirty work."

Then she left the kitchen. He found her a few minutes later in the living room with her feet up, staring into space.

Before he could sit or speak a single word, she began to talk. "Johnny had trouble with it sometimes. I could tell. Nightmares, mostly. Sometimes he'd just withdraw and not even want to be touched. It didn't happen often, but I could sense…changes. But it always passed quickly and then he'd be the old Johnny again." She turned her head toward him. "Every time he came back, I could feel that he'd changed some more. Life changes us all over time, but this was…different."

"It worried you?"

"Not exactly. It troubled me. Since he was killed, all I could remember were the good things. But they weren't always good, Ryker. God, I loved him, but I sometimes wondered what he was becoming."

He knew exactly what she meant. He could reach

back in his own mind and remember a young man who didn't carry so many dark secrets and stains on his soul. John had picked up those stains, too, and like acid they sometimes ate away at the soul.

He wished he knew what to tell her. He finally settled on, "Remember the good things, Marisa." Desperation struck him then. He didn't know where this was going, didn't know if he should clear out before it went any further. Wanting this woman wasn't enough. The question was if he had enough to give her.

When he saw her eyelids drooping again, he took advantage of it. "Take a nap. I'm going out for another run."

"Okay," she said drowsily. Then, "What are you running from, Ryker?"

He froze, but she was already asleep. He grabbed his jacket and left. What was he running from? Marisa Hayes and a future he didn't believe he had a right to.

Wasn't that enough?

Chapter Six

Ryker was doing laundry for Marisa. Much to her amazement, he not only knew how to do it, but he folded it beautifully. She'd let it go until she was down to her last clean underwear, and while it made her flush a little to think of him handling her intimate apparel, she had to admit she appreciated the help. Lately she'd been getting tired more often and napping more often, and the laundry looked like a daunting task.

It was Saturday morning, the day after Ryker had moved in, when Julie showed up unannounced.

"You need a change of scenery," Julie said. "We're going to my place, where I'm going to ply you with conversation and sinful food." She paused. "Is that Ryker in the basement? I saw his car out front."

"I asked him to move in. It was rude of me to keep him at the motel. Anyway, he's doing my laundry." She pointed to the basket on the floor beside the couch.

"You found a man who does laundry? Oh, be still, my beating heart!"

Marisa laughed.

"Just a sec." Julie went to the head of the stairs and called down. "Ryker?"

"Yo."

"I'm taking Marisa to my place for a change of scene."

"Go for it," came the answer. "When I'm through washing her stuff, I'm going to get to my own. She needs some time out of here."

"Don't I know it. Back in a few hours."

Ryker had freshly salted the porch and sidewalk, so the trip to Julie's car was safe enough. When they were inside, the engine running and the heater blowing, Julie asked, "Need to pick up anything while we're out?"

"I don't know. The guy moved in yesterday, he went grocery shopping, and I'm not even sure what he got, and he bought us dinner last night."

"Okay then." Julie smiled. "We'll call him before we come back to see if *he* needs anything. First, let's get to my place."

Julie had taken a ground floor apartment in one of the relatively new complexes that had been built during the brief boom of the semiconductor plant. The plant now sat sadly empty, the jobs had gone away, but the apartments remained.

She had a cheerful place, full of bright colors, impeccably clean except for stacks of papers and books on her coffee table and small desk from her teaching. She brewed a pot of tea after Marisa settled on an armchair, and brought it with some shortbread cookies.

"Now, dish," she said, her favorite line. "What did the doc say, and what is Ryker up to?"

"The doc says I'm nearly due."

Julie clattered the teapot as she put it down. "What?"

"You heard me. He thinks I got pregnant before my last period."

Julie sat down slowly. "Wow. Is that possible?"

"He says sometimes women have a light period when they first become pregnant. Well, it was light. And he added that he'd suspected when I first came to see him that I was farther along. I thought two months, he thought three. But he didn't say anything, because as he put it, it's hard to be sure. But now he thinks I'm getting pretty close."

Julie laughed. "Imagine the other girls dying of envy. Especially Connie. Her pregnancies always lasted ten months."

Marisa had to laugh, too. "I'd forgotten. Anyway, he said it's far from an exact science, that nine months is an approximation, but...he said there are signs. He's guessing just a few more weeks."

"How do you feel about it?" Julie settled and tucked her legs under her.

"I guess it's okay. I've been in stasis so long... God, Julie, I've been awful to everyone, and I'm so sorry."

"Cut it out," Julie said firmly. "You've been through a lot, and what kind of friends would we be if we didn't understand? Is that why you had Ryker move in?"

"Well, he'd be right there to drive me to the hospital."

Julie sipped her tea. "Have a cookie. Can I be perfectly frank?"

"Aren't you always?"

Julie sighed. "No. You know that. But I'm wondering about something."

Marisa tensed a little, but reached for a cookie. It gave

her something to occupy her hand and her mouth. Her heart thudded a bit as she wondered what was coming.

"This Ryker guy," Julie said. "A few weeks ago, you pushed him away. The *Do Not Disturb* signs were practically neon."

Marisa opened her mouth to explain, but Julie spoke first.

"The thing is, Marisa, maybe you don't know it, but I saw you eating him up with your eyes. You wanted that man."

"Oh, God." Marisa dropped the cookie on her saucer and felt a tear leak from one eye. She wanted to run and hide. "I'm awful."

"Awful?" Julie sounded startled. "What was awful? My God, I was so happy to see a stirring of life in you. I thought it was wonderful. Then you just shoved him away. Why?"

Marisa could barely shove the words out through her tightening throat. "It was wrong. Johnny…"

"Oh, to hell with that. You were grieving, sure. But that doesn't mean you can't live. You didn't have to crawl into that coffin with Johnny. Hell, none of us wanted to see that. We were worried about you. You just went into a cocoon and barely poked your nose out. So I got happy for you when you…showed some interest in something. A man. That's not a freaking crime!"

More tears rolled down Marisa's face, and she began to have trouble breathing. "I felt like it was."

"Well, it's not. And while we're on the subject, I want to remind you of something."

Marisa closed her eyes and nodded. Once Julie was on a roll, there was no stopping her. Even when it felt like taking it on the chin.

"Johnny was the one who left you. Over and over again he left you. Try to remember that. Then there's just one other thing before I shut my mouth. Go ahead and have a fling with Ryker if he's interested. You're entitled to some pleasure in your life. But damn it, just a fling, because he's another Johnny."

Ryker couldn't put Marisa's clothes away, so he left the basket beside her bed, awaiting her directions when she got home. Then he headed into the kitchen to start dinner for them, wondering if he should cook for Julie, as well.

But mostly he was wondering about himself. He felt yearnings he'd never felt before. Yearnings for a home, a family, all those ordinary things his life had kept from him. But unless he changed himself, he couldn't have any of them.

Quite a conundrum, he thought with bitter amusement. For years he'd been amazed that John had managed both, but then he'd been faced with Marisa. That was the price of his kind of life. Dying didn't begin to touch it. John had left devastation behind him in the life of a woman he loved. Maybe he'd never really thought it would happen. Or maybe he'd been so addicted to danger he simply couldn't quit.

But faced with the wreckage, Ryker couldn't consider adding any of those missing things to his life unless he was prepared to carve out a piece of himself. It just wouldn't be fair.

But when he tried to visualize himself in any other role, he faced a blank wall. He'd never been anything else. What would he replace it with? He couldn't imagine.

He'd never been given to a lot of self-reflection. As

a rule he was too busy, either on an assignment that took his full attention, or getting ready for one or coming back from one. Total job absorption. But since he'd learned about John, and mostly since he'd met John's wife, he had a hell of a lot to think about. Reevaluating himself proved to be an uncomfortable place to be.

Thus he was glad when he heard the front door open, heard Marisa's and Julie's voices.

"Welcome back," he called out.

But only Marisa came into the kitchen. She looked worn out, and he felt a spark of instant concern. "Something wrong? Where's Julie?"

"She had a meeting. I'm fine."

"Well, you don't look it," he said bluntly. "Go put your feet up. Want a glass of milk or something?"

She didn't answer, so he got her one, anyway. He found her in her bedroom, curled up on her bed. She hadn't even removed her jacket, although her gloves and scarf lay on the floor. The rules he had set for himself dictated that he just leave her alone. Well, to hell with the rules.

He entered the room, put the milk on her nightstand, then sat beside her. After a moment he caressed her arm. "Marisa? What happened? I thought you two were going to have fun."

"We did," she mumbled.

"Then what happened to fun?"

She didn't answer. He kept stroking her arm, hoping his touch felt soothing. Just as he was about to give up and leave her alone, she spoke.

"Julie said something that shook me up."

"What was that?"

"She pointed out to me that I had nothing to feel

guilty about. That I didn't leave Johnny, that he left me. That he was always leaving me."

He felt those words like a blow to his chest. They were painful to hear, and saying things about how it was John's job didn't take the sting out. He knew it. John had left her repeatedly, and not just to go to the corner store.

He continued to massage her arm gently, then did something totally uncharacteristic. He stretched out behind her and wrapped his arm around her. He wasn't accustomed to offering comfort, but strange as if felt, it was good. He just hoped it helped her in some small way. He also wondered if there was any way to convince her that John hadn't been leaving her. Because the truth was, year after year, John had gone away for months at a time, and he kept going away until he was unable to come home anymore.

Ryker was just the same. He had no business inserting himself into this woman's life, maybe giving her something else to worry about. Certainly no business holding her like this as if he could offer comfort when he was himself no comfort at all. Regardless of their earlier conversation, he needed to keep his distance. Protect her from a relationship of any kind that could leave her in the straits John had. Even friendship might be a danger to her.

But his world had been shaken, too. Here he was, holding a woman simply to offer comfort, and it felt magical. The lacks in is own life jolted his perspective, and he stared into emptiness over Marisa's head.

He felt her beginning to relax. Falling asleep? Maybe. He wondered if he should move anyway, get the hell out of this house and town.

Then she surprised him by murmuring, "I knew the

rules going in. Why did I let what Julie said upset me so much? It's not fair to John."

Now, that was a question indeed. His understanding of human nature was large but limited in scope. He wasn't used to dealing with the tenderer emotions. Not with things like this, and yet, here he was, comforting this woman with a hug, aware that lies would always stand between them and absolutely no understanding of what she was going through. He stifled a sigh and tried to think of one useful thing to offer. Some way to ease her. Because she didn't deserve this.

"Julie didn't mean it the way I took it," Marisa said after a short while. "I think she was encouraging me to get on with my own life. But…it hit me hard, Ryker. It was like looking at everything from a different angle."

Well, he understood that. It was happening to him right now, and no matter how hard he tried to straighten his head out, it remained all mixed up. He shoved himself aside to take care of Marisa. "Don't let this affect your memories," he said quietly. "Maybe all that's happening is that you're realizing you needed some things in your marriage that you didn't get. Probably pretty typical."

"Maybe."

"I mean, I'm no expert. Hell, I'm not even a beginner. I avoided all that. But I do know that John loved you. And I can guess how hard his absences must have been. But that doesn't diminish the love, does it?" He was floundering here and increasingly aware that he was building an internal list of all the things this woman deserved…and that didn't include being abandoned for months at a time or raising a kid without its father. John, he thought, you were one selfish jerk.

So he, too, was seeing things differently. Hitherto he'd thought John extremely lucky to have found a woman like Marisa. Now he was wondering if John had ever considered how much his chosen life had affected his wife.

Why the hell had Julie stirred up this hornet's nest? If he got the chance, he was going to ask her to explain herself.

Because at this point it seemed simply cruel, and Marisa had suffered enough cruelty.

As it turned out, he didn't have to wait long to confront Julie. Marisa fell asleep, and he slipped from her side to let her rest comfortably. He was in the kitchen putting together dinner when he heard a car pull up.

Going to the front, he saw it was Julie. He grabbed his jacket and stepped out into the icy air, watching the woman approach him.

"She's sleeping," he said shortly, without greeting.

Julie studied him from green eyes. "Who made you the castle gatekeeper?"

"Me."

Julie nodded slowly, and he couldn't understand why a smile tugged at the corners of her mouth. "So, you're another Johnny?"

He didn't deny it. Instead, he went on the attack. "Why'd you upset her?"

Julie's face changed, the hinted smile evaporating. "What do you mean?"

"Telling her that John was always leaving her. It upset her. It's making her question everything."

"Ah, hell." Julie looked away, stuffing her hands into the pockets of her coat. "I was afraid of that." Her breath blew clouds on the frigid air. "I was just trying to tell her that she had a right to move on. That she wasn't betraying Johnny in some way if she did. After all, he kept walking out that door. She ought to be able to walk forward, at least." She turned her attention back to Ryker. "She's attracted to you."

He didn't reply.

"Go ahead and be a sphinx. But I have some words for you. Don't you dare hurt her. If you're planning to treat her the way Johnny did, then get the hell out right now. It's not right for her to keep living her life waiting for a man to come home. Not right at all. And love doesn't make it right."

Wow, he thought as he watched her walk back to her car. That woman didn't pull her punches. "Julie?" he called.

She turned with obvious reluctance.

"Thanks for being such a good friend to her."

At that Julie moved toward him. He came down the steps so he didn't tower over her.

"I don't know what's with you," she said. "You were Johnny's friend, so I presume you lead the same kind of life. She loved that man. I don't want to see her in this position again. And now there's a kid to concern me, too. You might be a nice guy, for all I know. Just don't drag her and that kid back into limbo. Don't."

He nodded once. "I read you. And that's not my intention at all."

"Intentions are meaningless. Actions count. She's not one to bark and snarl, but I am."

Again he nodded. "Thing is, she makes her own decisions. What worries me is that you made her hurt."

"Yeah." Julie blew a sigh, a white cloud. "I didn't

mean it that way. I really didn't. I know she's attracted to you. I was kind of trying to give her a blessing, so she wouldn't feel guilty about it. But on the other hand… No more Johnnys."

This time he let her go. She hadn't said one thing he didn't already know. Whatever he did, whatever Marisa chose, he had to ensure he didn't put her back where she'd been.

The question was, could *he* change? Because he definitely didn't want to make Marisa change. Or maybe the better question was simply whether he should just clear out of here after the baby came. She'd have plenty of girlfriends to help her out, women who knew a helluva lot more about babies than he.

As he was combining ingredients for a pot roast, he suddenly froze and wondered why the hell he was even thinking of such things. Soon he'd hit the road again, go back to his life and leave Marisa behind in hers.

Some questions didn't need answers. In fact, they shouldn't even be asked.

Marisa's nap revived her. She awoke to a house full of delicious aromas, then suddenly remembered she had fallen asleep with Ryker holding her. Okay, the guy could be sweet. Even understanding. But he was still a box full of secrets, and really, she'd had enough of that. Julie could say whatever she wanted about a fling being okay, but Marisa wasn't buying it.

She wasn't the "fling" type. Johnny had been her one and only, and with her looming responsibilities to a child, she'd be a fool to change that.

Rising, she freshened up, then headed toward the front of the house to find out what was going on. Ryker was sitting on the couch, reading a book. He looked up and smiled.

"Feeling better?"

"Much. I don't know what got into Julie."

He put the book aside. "I do. She came by while you were sleeping. Apparently, she was trying to tell you to seize the day and then realized later that you might have taken it wrong. She also had a message for me."

Marisa slowly perched on the other end of the couch. "What is she doing messing in my life like this?"

"Being a friend," he said truthfully.

"So, what was her message for you?"

"That I'll be drawn and quartered if I harm a hair on your head."

At first Marisa gasped, then a laugh spilled out of her. The baby stirred, kicking hard. "She'd never have said such a thing."

"Not exactly in those words."

Marisa laid a hand over her stomach, feeling the pokes and prods. Nobody had shared this with her. Nobody. And all of a sudden she had a crying need to share it with someone.

"Come here," she said. "Just scoot closer."

His gaze narrowed a bit, but he did as asked. Then she took his large hand and pressed it to her belly. "Just feel her."

He drew a breath. "Wow," he murmured.

"Wait. Sometimes it feels like she's turning over in there."

He closed his eyes, waiting as she had asked. "Such life," he said quietly. "So much life."

His eyes opened and met hers squarely. She felt electricity zap between them, as if she'd just been connected to a battery. Then every cell in her began to hum with desire. She wanted this man. He might be trouble, but she wanted him, anyway.

Not good, she reminded herself. Ryker would soon leave. He had a job to get back to, a whole life buried in the secrets he and Johnny couldn't share with her. But for now...for now she needed someone to share her joy in this growing baby. Put everything else on the back burner, just savor this moment, a moment she should have been sharing with her husband. Sharing it with his friend at least assuaged some of her need.

"What do I smell cooking?" she asked eventually.

"Pot roast. I hope it's not too salty."

"I'll drink a lot of water."

He removed his hand, then clasped hers. "Marisa? That was special. Thanks for sharing with me."

"Well, I can't share it with Johnny." She meant to say it lightly, but it came out sounding rather different.

Ryker stood up. "I'm not Johnny." He was halfway to the kitchen when he called back, "You want water or something?"

"I'll get it." She sat there feeling almost stunned. The way he had said *I'm not Johnny.* It had sounded angry. Maybe bitter. What the hell was going on now?

She waited a while, trying to compose herself, running her palms over her tummy in a soothing motion that probably did more for her than her baby. Eventually, however, she needed a drink and had to venture into the kitchen, where Ryker seemed to have ensconced himself.

He was seated at the table, staring out the window at the wintry day. Snowflakes had begun to fall, and she wondered vaguely how much accumulation they'd get.

She went to the refrigerator for a glass of orange juice, then paused. "Dinner smells really good," she offered.

"Thanks."

Okay, this wasn't working. "What did Julie say to you exactly?"

"Only the truth," he said grudgingly.

"Which was?"

"That you don't need another Johnny."

Marisa caught her breath and felt her heart slam. "She had no right…"

"She's your friend. She's concerned about you. She has every right."

She pulled out a chair and sat facing him. Standing too long these days made her back ache a bit. "You'd think the back muscles would keep up with the pregnancy," she remarked.

That drew his attention toward her.

"Meaning?"

"Apparently, they don't. I can't stand for long now without my back aching. It's mostly mild, but why flirt with a bigger problem?"

"Oh." He drummed his fingers lightly. "I'm sorry if I upset you more."

"You didn't upset me, you confused me and made me wonder what Julie said to you. I know you're not Johnny."

"I didn't quite mean it that way." But maybe he meant it in the most important ways. "I told you I want you. I know you want me. That's ordinary human interaction. Feeling desire is normal. We all do. What concerns me is… I don't want to do anything that might hurt you. However accidentally. From the way Julie tells it, you're finally emerging from your cocoon. I'd like to help with that, not drive you back into it."

Marisa nodded slowly, running her finger along the side of her orange juice glass, collecting condensation. The ache was returning, and this time it wasn't sexual. She felt as if another loss hovered right around the corner. "Are you telling me you're not trustworthy?"

"Depends," he answered shortly.

"On what?"

"Whether I can provide what's needed." His face darkened, and she thought he looked almost frightening. "Tell me to take a hike and I'll expend my last drop of blood to do it. But this…you… You need things I've never had to provide. Never even *tried* to provide."

"Sheesh, Ryker, what does it matter? You don't know what I need, and I'm not asking you for anything, anyway." Her heart was racing now, feeling something important was going on, but danged if she knew what. This guy had barely entered her life. Whether she wanted him sexually was irrelevant. They didn't exactly have a relationship for him to be worrying about.

"It matters," he said. "Because I'm not going to turn you into a casual conquest. You deserve better. And whether or not you want it from me, I still need to know if I can give it. So forget casual. Forget a fling. It ain't gonna happen. I care too much." He shook his head as if to shake something loose. "I care too much," he repeated quietly. "And that's the hell of it. Never did that before, either."

He stood up. "Another hour or so on the slow cooker. I'm going out."

She looked up at him. "Will you be back?"

"Hell if I know."

Then he was gone, leaving her alone in the silent, empty house, the only trace of him the aromas from the slow cooker. What had just happened?

She pushed her orange juice to one side and put her head down the table. Hot tears burned in her eyes and fell on her hands.

She cared, too. *I'm so sorry, Johnny,* she thought. *I didn't want to betray you.* It hadn't even been a year. Not even a year, and already she was somehow crazily tangled up with another man. And it was crazy. Ryker? Who the hell was Ryker? Would she ever know? Did it matter?

She gave in to the tears, just let herself sob them all out. She'd been safer in her cocoon of grief, but somehow Ryker had yanked her out of it, making life all too close again. No muffling between her and it. She was smack-dab back in all the confusion, pain and upset of being alive.

And this time it wasn't grief.

Chapter Seven

Ryker drove for hours along back country roads, feeling as if a Pandora's box had been opened inside him. All the soul-searching he'd failed to do over the years, all the decisions he'd made or had refused to make, the truncated personality he'd become...they all leaped out and screamed at him like unleashed Furies.

Why the hell had John Hayes asked this of him? More than anyone else on the planet, John had to have been aware of Ryker's lacks. His narrow set of emotions. The secrets that would always stand between him and anyone else.

"What were you thinking, John?" But of course there was no answer. Of all the people John could have asked to check on his wife if anything happened, there were a million better choices than Ryker.

John had chosen to lay this on Ryker, and now that

the baby was imminent, Ryker knew he couldn't leave. Not yet. But that was no excuse for what John had caused here, because John hadn't known about the kid.

Or maybe John had been just that selfish. Maybe he hadn't understood Ryker at all. After all, his friend was the one who'd kept leaving a wife behind time and again to go on dangerous missions until he got himself killed. The guy who wouldn't leave the Rangers until he got himself a dangerous covert job with the CIA.

Ryker could hardly hold himself blameless, though. He hadn't *had* to get John that job. He could have told the guy to go home and settle down. But, maybe just like John, he hadn't given any thought to Marisa. She wasn't *his* wife. What did it matter to him?

Oh, hell, it mattered. It mattered in ways he wasn't used to and didn't know how to handle. Or even sort out.

What did John think Ryker would do? Pull into town, make a little recon, find out if Marisa needed anything, then head out again?

Cussing, Ryker turned into the parking lot of a road-house and slammed the car into Park. Maybe that was the Ryker John thought he knew. A man who could come here and leave everything untouched. Leave Marisa in her misery. Barely touch the edges of her consciousness. A gesture, nothing more. A way to speak from beyond the grave and remind this woman he'd loved her.

Well, it hadn't worked that way, had it? What's more, he was beginning to agree with Julie's unspoken assessment of John. Selfish and always walking out the door.

The ugliest thought popped into his head. John had known Ryker wouldn't be able to make it until months after the funeral. Maybe this had been John's way of keeping her grief fresh, of keeping her to himself, because he knew Ryker's rule on women.

Could that man have really been so ugly inside?

It was possible, much as he hated to believe it. But he knew as well how much the kind of life they led could breed ugliness in some. And how possessive some men could be.

He cussed again and switched off the car, heading inside to get a beer. Just one, because he had to get back to that house to look after Marisa. John's other legacy. One that was probably turning out very differently than John had expected.

Ryker tried to shake the thought away. Maybe John had been trying to make a point to Ryker. It was possible. He'd often tried to persuade Ryker that marriage was a good thing.

Ryker was having none of it. And after seeing what it had cost Marisa, he was having even less of it.

He'd have to change himself in ways he could scarcely imagine before he would feel right about sharing his life with a woman.

And that was that.

Ryker was gone so long that Marisa finally helped herself to a small bowl of pot roast, then went into the living room to watch whatever was on TV. She loved to read, but lately reading put her quickly to sleep, and she didn't want to sleep. Not again and not yet.

She found a sitcom rerun and left it on for some background noise. When she glanced out the window, she saw that it was snowing again, a little harder than earlier. She hoped Ryker was safe on the roads.

With her hands resting on her tummy, feeling the

occasional movements of her child, she tried to parse through what had happened that day.

First, Julie had encouraged her to have an affair. Then, she'd apparently come over here to warn Ryker off. Why?

And what had put Ryker in such a turmoil? Why should he be worrying about whether he could provide what she needed? He was just passing through. A friend of Johnny's performing a duty.

That was it, and the sexual attraction that had flared between them didn't change any of that.

Regardless, she got the feeling that something was tearing Ryker apart, and she couldn't imagine what or why. It certainly couldn't be her. He'd been up front with her about his casual approach to women. *Love 'em and leave 'em*, he'd said. Very uncomplicated.

She wondered if she could handle that kind of uncomplicated, or if it would somehow become complicated for her. She had no way to know.

She *did* realize that she was feeling badly for Ryker, though. She sensed that Johnny had somehow put him in an untenable situation. Should she try to get him to talk honestly about it, or was it better just to leave it alone?

But one thing she knew for sure—the clear-eyed, decisive man who had arrived here had vanished. Troubles lurked in his gaze the way they had in hers for so long. Troubles like that didn't go away overnight, as she ought to know.

Emerging from her grief was proving painful in its own way, and she wondered if Ryker was experiencing something like that. He'd been Johnny's friend, after all.

Speculating wasn't at all helpful, though. Not at all. She'd thought Ryker was a man full of secrets, like

Johnny, and he was. But different from Johnny. Johnny had mostly seemed untroubled. Ryker was striking her as a man who was being ripped apart from the inside by something.

At long last she heard him come back.

"I'm in the living room," she called. Lying on the couch with her feet up. She reached for the remote and turned off the TV, hoping he'd join her. She was done with solitude, she realized.

"Hi," he said. "How was dinner?"

"Fabulous. Get yourself some." She turned her head just a little, catching only a glimpse of him in the doorway.

"I wanted to put your laundry away, but you have to tell me where."

"Later. It can wait. You folded it so neatly it seems a shame to disturb it. Eat something."

Five minutes later he returned with his dinner in a bowl. He took the rocker across from her and started eating. "You've been okay?"

She snorted. "It may surprise the world, but I've been breathing successfully on my own for over thirty-two years."

He flashed a grin at her, then resumed eating. Between mouthfuls, he spoke. "I've been driving around. Beautiful country here."

"I got a little worried when I saw the snow was growing heavier."

"The roads are getting slick," he agreed. "There is, however, a roadhouse that I'd advise you to avoid if you should ever get the urge."

She pushed herself up against the arm of the couch. "Did something happen?"

"No, I didn't let it happen. I stopped to get a beer, and you could say the atmosphere changed."

She blinked. "But why?"

"Look at me, Marisa. I learned long ago that something about me seems to challenge other men. Not all of them, but some. So I drank half my beer, gave them my best killer look and got the hell out. Some help I'd be to you sitting in a cell for brawling in a bar."

She put her hand to her mouth, afraid she might smile at the silliness. "Really?"

"Really. It happens. I don't know what it is. Anyway, nothing occurred, so it's unimportant."

"Have you ever brawled?"

"Hell, yeah. Sometimes you can't avoid it."

She nodded slowly. "Johnny told me about one or two."

"See? Put a little alcohol in some guys and they suddenly start looking for a place to plant their fists."

"But not you?"

He looked up again. "I told you. I don't have anything to prove."

He resumed eating. She bit her lip, then decided to risk it.

"Why did Johnny ask you to check on me?"

He scraped the last bit from his bowl and set it aside. "I told you I don't know. I've been wondering the same thing. Why?"

"Because you seem so uncomfortable."

"Sometimes I am," he admitted frankly. "I took care of my men, but that's a whole different thing from looking after you. John knew that. He knew I had little to do with women, except casually. Call me stunted. I guess I am. So I don't have a clue."

"But this doesn't seem fair to you."

"Fair?" He arched a brow at her. "Really? You know fair doesn't enter into it."

"But I can tell…something about me is making you uncomfortable."

"Wrong." One single word. A few seconds passed before he elaborated. "You're not causing my problem. You may have made me aware, but you didn't cause this. I'm trying to figure out how to relate to a world I haven't been part of since I was a kid. Change is always uncomfortable, but maybe it's time I made a few. Haven't decided what yet, but there it is. I'm shedding a skin, I guess…growing, I hope. But I'm not sure of much right now."

"You don't need to do this."

His black eyes bored into her. "Actually, I think I do."

His gaze made her heart speed up. Almost as if he reached out physically and touched her, she felt desire begin to drizzle through her entire body, hot and exciting. "Is that what you decided while you were out?" She hoped she didn't sound as breathless as she felt.

"Not exactly. Let's just say I accepted it. Something about walking into that bar. Déjà vu all over again, as they say. I'd been there before, too many times, all over the world. The threat creeping up my neck as eyes fixed on me. My entire body crawling with adrenaline as I waited for it to happen. I'm tired of it."

Well, that was one amazing statement, she thought as she studied him. Tired of it? But it was his life. She'd thought Johnny was making a huge change when he moved out of the army to the State Department, but apparently not. Not considering that he had been killed. Not considering what Ryker had just said. Did the State

Department put people in harm's way as if they were soldiers? Or were there just some jobs... She stopped herself. She'd never know. That had been made abundantly clear to her. Ask as she might, no one would tell her exactly what had happened, what Johnny had been doing. No street mugging, of that she was certain, but what if he'd been doing something decidedly more dangerous? What if all he'd done was find another way to live on the edge he loved?

She sighed, twisted her fingers together and looked at them. Somehow she just had to let go of all that. No amount of knowledge would ease the loss. "What would you do?" she asked suddenly.

"What?" He sounded surprised, as if his mind had moved on.

"If you left your current job?"

"I don't know," he said frankly. "I have a lot of skills that are useless in the civilian world. Well, mostly useless. Occasionally I've toyed with running a survival school or becoming a hunting guide. What I couldn't do is plant myself behind a desk."

In that instant, a light of understanding flared in Marisa's mind. No desk job. State Department? He said he'd run security. Wouldn't that mostly be a desk job? What the hell had Johnny been doing? Because all of a sudden, her imaginings evaporated, and she knew with certainty that Johnny hadn't taken a desk job, either. He hadn't been sitting in some cozy little embassy or consulate somewhere doing routine translations. That wouldn't have suited him at all.

"Ryker? Johnny didn't have a desk job, did he?"

His gaze grew hollow, but he didn't answer.

"What the hell was he doing?"

"I know exactly what they told you. Not one thing more."

"But you know more about the kind of work." Angry now, she struggled to her feet and began pacing. "Everyone's lying to me. Everyone, and that includes Johnny. My God, I can't believe he let me ramble on with all my excited imaginings about the exotic places we could visit with the State Department! He knew I'd never go with him, didn't he? Didn't he, Ryker?" She faced him.

He just shook his head. "I don't know what he thought."

"But you know what he did. And that didn't include bringing a family."

"Actually," he said, rising, "I *don't* know what he was doing. I can't even find out!"

She glared at him, then turned her back on him, accepting that in this, at least, he was telling the truth. "Secrets," she said bitterly. "So many secrets. Did I even know my own husband?"

She felt his hand grip her shoulder gently. She half wanted to shake free and half wanted to turn into his arms.

"You knew the man he was when he was with you," he said quietly. "That's the only part that matters."

"Really? How many lies did he tell me?"

His grip tightened a bit. "I know he loved you. So he never lied to you about that or about your relationship."

"But he never told me anything about what he did, and now I'll never know, and that was such a big part of his life. Now there's you, the same secrets, only you're sweating them. Wanting to change. Johnny never wanted to change."

He turned her then, wrapping his powerful arms

around her, holding her close. Clearly he had no answer for her, but right at that moment she was simply grateful to have someone holding her, because inside she felt herself shattering into a million pieces. Who had she been married to?

His chest rumbled beneath her ear as he spoke. "He was a good man, Marisa. He loved you. A little reckless, maybe, but a good man. I'm sorry I can't tell you any more. I warned you from the beginning, there are operational secrets. Johnny told you that, too. I don't know what Johnny was doing or what his mission was when he died."

But her mind was already straying in a different direction. God, it had been so long since she'd been held like this, comforted like this. Not even knowing that Ryker was just another man full of secrets could change the way he was making her feel: cared for, protected, supported. She'd been alone and lonely for way too long.

She was also pregnant, and before long, leaning into him was making her lower back ache. She didn't want to pull away, but as the ache grew, she knew she had to.

It was almost as if he read her mind. He let go of her, gently eased her back onto the couch, then sat beside her, lifting her legs so his lap cradled them.

"Comfortable?" he asked as she leaned back against the armrest.

"Thanks." It was the best she could manage when she felt as if her insides had been shredded. When Johnny had been in the Rangers, she'd had some idea of what he was doing. He was a soldier, and he went on dangerous missions. When he'd joined the State Department, she'd apparently built castles in the air that had nothing whatsoever to do with reality. Living proof now held her legs in his lap.

With strong hands he began to knead her lower legs through her fleece pants. It felt so good she couldn't have stopped him. Life seemed to be shattering and flying in a million directions, and from what he'd said, he was feeling much the same. What was going on here?

But she was growing awfully tired of unanswered and unanswerable questions.

"I'm sorry I don't have your answers," he said a while later.

"That's not your fault, is it? I'm beginning to really get it."

"In what way?" His hands continued their soothing motions.

"You don't know a whole lot more than I do. Oh, you know what *you* were doing but little else."

He didn't answer immediately, then remarked, "We call it compartmentalizing. Need to know. Each little part is separate from all the other parts."

That was probably the single most revealing thing he'd told her. "So you operate in the dark, too?"

"Much of the time. I know only what I need to."

"Does that seem right to you?"

He turned, his dark eyes catching hers. "It used to."

An interesting choice of phrase. She seized on it, hoping she wouldn't regret pressing him. "And now?"

"Now?" He looked away, still massaging her legs. "I don't know. Maybe there are too many widows like you who don't know the very things they should have a right to know. I couldn't tell you."

"Because you don't know."

"Exactly." His hands paused, then resumed the massage. "It's part of what I've been thinking about, Marisa. I've lived most of my life in the shadows. Do I want to live the rest of it that way? Maybe die in the shadows the way John did? I don't know anymore. And maybe that's why John sent me here."

"What do you mean? You said he loved his work."

"He did. But maybe, like me, he was starting to have second thoughts. I don't know. Maybe he sensed I was having them. Maybe he just wanted me to stop and think about all I was missing. I couldn't read his mind then, and I sure as hell can't read it now. Regardless, he only asked me to check on you if something happened to him. He couldn't have known it would, so all the rest is just speculation and probably had nothing to do with it."

But she sensed a change in him, a slight stiffening. She ran his words back through her mind and then said, her voice taut, her chest so tight she could scarcely force the words out, "He knew."

His head turned sharply. "Knew?"

"Knew he was going to die."

"Marisa…"

"I had a friend in high school. They were on a trip. She told her mother if she didn't go home immediately, she'd never go home again. The next day she drowned." She squeezed her eyes shut. "Sometimes people know," she whispered.

When Ryker didn't argue with her, she opened her eyes again. "You know it, too, don't you? That some people seem to know before…"

"I've seen it," he admitted. "Not often, but I've seen it."

"So when, exactly, did John make you promise to check on me?"

His voice was heavy when he answered. "Right after I got him the job."

Marisa turned her head, looking out the window at the falling snow. The winter night had fully settled in, and the flakes glistened in the light from the street lamp and windows. She felt as if snow was falling inside her, too, frigid and cold. But like the flakes outside, the flakes inside were ephemeral, beautiful at first blush, but doomed to vanish at the first warmth.

She was thawing, she realized. She'd been frozen ever since she'd learned of Johnny's death. Now all her pretty little dreams and thoughts were melting, going the way those snowflakes would go eventually. Fleeting. Impermanent.

Her baby stirred, and she pressed her hands to the mound of her tummy. That was real, but was anything else? Her baby. All she had left of a marriage that had apparently been like a snowfall.

Ryker's hands paused on her legs. "Marisa?"

When she didn't answer, he moved. With astonishing ease, ungainly though she felt right then, he twisted and lifted her until he could settle her sideways on his lap. He wrapped both arms around her and just held her.

"I guess I was the wrong guy to send," he said finally.

"Why?"

"Because we're both messed up. I'm no help at all."

She thought about that, about the awakening happening inside her, about the baby that had just decided to become rambunctious, so much so that, without asking, Ryker loosened one of his arms and rested his hand on her belly.

"Hello, Jonni," he murmured.

She looked down at his big hand pressed gently to

her stomach. Life. Maybe most of it was ephemeral but not the little girl growing inside her.

With her head resting on Ryker's shoulder, she thought about the last time she'd seen Johnny. He'd been home for just over two months. When he'd kissed her goodbye and sworn he'd miss her every moment, she hadn't missed the excitement dancing in his gaze. He was glad to be off again. Going on another dangerous adventure. Unaware of the child he was leaving behind.

"Johnny," she said slowly, "never settled down. Never. He never would. If he hadn't died…" Her voice caught, then steadied. "He wouldn't have been home for this," she said. "He wouldn't have. I'd have gone through this entire pregnancy alone. Just the way I have. Until you arrived."

"Marisa…"

"That's why he sent you. At some level he knew he wouldn't be here when I needed him most."

She felt Ryker shake his head, but she knew it in the depths of her being. It was true. The baby was Johnny's legacy, but Ryker was his last gift. She didn't know what to make of that.

"He was doing important work," Ryker offered.

"I'm sure. I never doubted that. But he lived to exist on the edge, Ryker. I knew that, too. What about you? Do you need to be on the edge all the time?"

He blew a long breath. "I think I just told you that's changing."

"Yes, you did. But for how long? How real is it?"

He gently rubbed his hand over her belly. "As real as this child. My gut's saying so."

"And then what?"

"I don't know," he said frankly. "I told you that, too.

I just know I've enjoyed hanging around this town for the last month. I thought I'd be bored, but I haven't been. Nice folks for the most part. I walk down the street without having to be on high alert. People are starting to greet me. I've had some casual conversations where I didn't have to guard every word. It's been like letting go of a suffocating weight."

Her heart hurt as realization sank in. "I feel like I'm waking up from a bad dream that went on forever." Her eyes burned, and she felt one tear roll down her cheek. "I spent most of my marriage missing Johnny. I can't do that again."

"No one's asking you to."

"I know. It's just…I wonder at myself. Why my perspective is changing so much. I thought I'd accepted the way things had to be. Not so much, I guess. I might have lived an illusion for years. But one thing I know for sure now…I loved him. Part of me will always love him, but I cannot do that again. I have a child to think of now, to care for. I need some permanence and stability. Johnny never would have provided that. So it's time to leave all that in the past. Time to look forward and plan. High time."

Ryker lifted his hand and with a finger wiped away the one tear. "Don't give him up, Marisa. He loved you. Keep that part of him."

"I'll never lose that." She closed her eyes, dropped her head and placed her hand over Ryker's. "Nothing can take it away from me. But I'm through railing at the universe and hating life and all the rest of it. Johnny was a bright and beautiful addition to my life. But he wasn't all of it." He hadn't been around enough to be all of it.

She lifted a hand and laid it on Ryker's chest. Through

the flannel of his shirt she could feel heat and hard muscle. Reality.

"No one person," he said slowly, "should be all of someone's life."

"Probably not. I don't mean it as a criticism of Johnny. Like I said, I knew what it would be like. I'm just looking at myself and wondering how much longer I'm going to wallow in missing him. It seems almost like copping out."

"To hell with that," he said sharply. "The man you loved died. Whether he was around much before that hardly matters. This time he's not coming back. A bit weird, don't you think, to dismiss your grief because he wasn't around often? There's a huge difference between temporary and permanent."

And therein resided a huge kernel of truth. Johnny would never come home, and she grieved for that. She grieved because she could no longer look forward to those amazing, bright spots of love that had filled her days when he was here. She had every right to miss him.

But it was dawning on her that she had every right to move on.

Chapter Eight

"It's almost Christmas," Ryker remarked the next morning as they sat over coffee and the eggs he'd made for them.

"So?"

He glanced out the window at falling snow, then at her. "What did you do for Thanksgiving?"

"Stayed home."

He arched a brow. "Really? I'm surprised. All those friends threw you a baby shower."

"And all those friends asked me to join them for Thanksgiving. I said no."

He studied her, drumming his fingers. "How come?"

"Do you really think I wanted to be surrounded by all their families and friends?"

Ryker studied her, beginning to understand something. He wondered if she had any idea how cute she looked with her hair still tousled from bed, wrapped in a pink terry-cloth robe over what appeared to be thermal underwear. Or how bright her almost-lavender eyes looked? Appealing in every way. "Explain," he suggested gently.

"I would have just felt more alone. I can't explain it any better than that."

She sounded a bit querulous now. He felt one corner of his mouth twitch upward. She was definitely shaking free of the paralysis that had been plaguing her when he arrived. Good. Time to tiptoe, though. He was aware that he felt uniquely exposed here, as if his long-protected and buried feelings were now running around out in the world and vulnerable. She was probably feeling the same.

"What did *you* do for Thanksgiving?" she demanded.

"Called my parents. And Maude makes a mean turkey dinner."

"Hah," she said. "Another loner." Then, "Why didn't you go visit your parents?"

"They don't expect me anymore, and…" Did he really want to tell her this? "Frankly, I don't feel comfortable with them. It would have been three or four days of being badgered about the way I live."

Marisa concerned him more. She was truly out of sorts this morning, maybe not surprising, given the thoughts she'd expressed last night, but he had no idea how to soothe her. Damn, he was getting too involved here. Why should he care that she was having a mood? Why should he feel he needed to do something about it? But he did. He just had to feel his way into it. He poured himself another coffee and returned to the table, pondering.

He asked, "Was John home last Christmas?"

"No. He came in February."

"Well, I wasn't home last Christmas either, just like Thanksgiving. In fact, it's been years since I was anywhere near Christmas."

"So?"

He hesitated, then jumped in with both feet. What the hell? He'd been tongue-lashed before. "I want to ask a favor."

She almost scowled at him. "What?"

"Can I get a tree? Some trimmings? Would you mind?"

Some of the irritability vanished from her face. Her mouth opened a bit. "For you, you mean?"

"Yeah. For me." But not just for him. No way. He knew loneliness intimately, and he figured this woman had had her share and then some.

"I have an artificial tree in the attic. Decorations. Help yourself."

"I was thinking of a real tree, unless you object. The scent of pine. God, I love that." He waited. He was proposing to celebrate a holiday in her house, and he'd just dismissed her usual decorations for something entirely different. He knew he needed a change. He wondered if she was ready to really make one.

So much to hang on one Christmas tree, he thought with self-amusement.

"Sure," she said after a minute. "Go ahead."

"Want to tell me where to put it? And better yet, help me pick it out? It's going to be in your house, after all."

Her lips curved, but the smile didn't appear especially amused. "What are you trying to do, Ryker?"

"Change up my life. God knows it needs changing. The last time I decorated a Christmas tree was nearly twenty years ago. In a forward base in the middle of no-where. This scrawny thing we decorated with whatever crap we could find lying around."

She continued to regard him, apparently thinking. Slowly, she relaxed a bit. "Sure," she said finally. "Go ahead. Just don't expect me to get all into it."

"This tree's for me," he reminded her. "If you want your own, I'll get it out of your attic."

That worked. A laugh escaped her, a genuine one. "You are too much," she told him. "One tree is plenty. Yours will be plenty."

And maybe it would help put a different complexion on things for both of them. He'd just have to wait and see.

"Whenever you're ready to bundle up," he said, of-fering a smile. "Dang, I'm getting excited."

"About Christmas?" She laughed again. "Still a kid inside?"

"I think the kid inside me has been locked away for too long."

Her face softened, and she surprised him by reaching across the table for his hand. "Then, let's let the kid out."

She insisted on doing the dishes, so while she cleaned up and dressed to go out, he shoveled the fresh snowfall off her steps and sidewalks. Only a few inches of light and fluffy stuff made it easy. Then he salted every place she might have to walk, brushed off his car and started it to warm it up.

Other people were out shoveling, too, and he liked the way they waved to him, as if he were part of the neigh-borhood now. Friendly folks. He'd been running into that everywhere. Quite a change from his past.

Streets he could walk without feeling exposed. People

with nothing deadly to hide. Something inside him was uncoiling in response, and only as he began to relax into his new environment did he realize how long it had been since he'd simply felt comfortable in any environment.

Yeah, they gave him decompression time after every mission, but looking back now he could easily see that he had never fully decompressed. Too afraid of losing his edge.

Here, somehow, that didn't seem important. He might be making a big mistake, but he didn't care. Life had finally delivered him a small measure of peace, and he made up his mind to enjoy it.

Once he had Marisa safely bundled into his car, he drove them toward a tree lot he'd seen yesterday on the edge of town. Even though Thanksgiving had passed, it had still appeared to have quite a few decent trees in it. A mental checklist began to run of all the other things he'd need to get, from a tree stand to some ornaments. Maybe some lights for outside?

It would depend, he decided, on Marisa's reactions. If she seemed to be enjoying herself, he'd go whole hog on it.

Although it had been plowed, the parking around the tree lot was still covered with snow. No one else was there this morning, except for an older man inside a little hut with a propane space heater. With Marisa's arm firmly tucked in his for support, they began to walk around the narrow paths in the small lot.

"Any particular kind of tree you favor?" he asked her.

"This is your tree."

"I'm kinda out of practice. I'm just asking what you think is pretty."

She glanced at him with a smile. "I like the long-needled ones because they look full. On the other hand, the short-needled ones are sparser-looking but can hold a lot more decorations."

"Some help you are."

She laughed, and he soaked up the sound. "How high are your ceilings?" He figured close to ten feet. It was an older house.

"High enough. The thing is, we can't get a humongous tree unless you want to move furniture onto the front porch."

"Good point. I guess I shouldn't go overboard."

"Just saying." Then she laughed again. She was enjoying this. He could have given himself a pat on the back.

"I never went tree shopping with Johnny."

He almost froze, then caught himself. "Never?" The thought that she'd had to deal with holidays on her own struck him for the first time. Of course she had an artificial tree in the attic. He'd almost have bet that some years she didn't even get it down.

Cripes. They strolled a little farther, then he heard Marisa draw a sharp breath. At once he stopped and turned to her. "You okay?"

"I'm fine." She was staring past him, so he looked and saw the tree that held her attention. In an instant it became The Tree.

"You like that one?"

"I've always loved blue spruce. I've never had one for a Christmas tree."

He studied it. Six feet tall, thick foliage and surprisingly blue compared to the trees around it. "That's wild. I like it."

"Are you sure?"

He'd been sure since he'd seen the sparkle in her eyes.

He didn't care if it was full all the way around, or anything else. If it had bare spots, they had plenty of walls to hide them against. Glancing around, he saw no others of its kind.

"Okay, let's get you back to the car, then I'll help the guy load it up."

She hesitated. "Don't do this for me."

"Did I say I was? I like it, too. It's different."

He was glad she didn't argue. He understood that she wanted to think this was all about him, and to some extent it was. He didn't want to be pushed into a corner where he had to admit he was doing this mostly for her, to break a cycle, because he was nearly certain that would make her uneasy.

But it was time, with the baby's arrival so near, for this woman to find some happiness in life again.

By that evening, Ryker had the tree standing in the corner of the living room and was stringing it with multicolored lights. Marisa sat with her feet up, watching him and thinking that he finally looked relaxed and content.

If she were to be honest, she was feeling pretty relaxed and content herself. Her baby stirred comfortably in her womb, a Christmas tree was happening right before her eyes, and she spared only a few minutes to think about how she had missed doing this with Johnny. Only once in their marriage had he been home to participate in this. But then she let go of the regret and gave herself over to enjoying Ryker. As he handled the strings of lights, he even taught her a few new cusswords that made her giggle.

"I forgot this was the miserable part," he said at one point. "Sorry."

"No apologies. I'm having too much fun watching."

He pretended to scowl at her as he wound the light strands around the tree. "I hope all the same colors don't wind up in one place."

"You got a problem with blotches?"

"Not unless it means I have to do this all over again."

She laughed again. On one of his trips out for ornaments, he'd brought home dinner again, so she didn't even need to cook. She was beginning to feel like a lady of leisure.

He flashed a smile at her. "You're enjoying watching a tree torture me, huh?"

"Believe it."

On the floor lay boxes of ornaments he'd purchased. She liked their bright colors but was surprised he hadn't purchased any glass ones. Was he thinking of the baby to come? Most were brass or decorated foam, pretty indestructible. Or maybe that was just the way he thought.

"Want some coffee?" she asked.

He left the light strand dangling. "I'll get it. I need a break. I am at war with this tree. You want anything?"

"Milk would be nice. I thought you were going to have fun with this."

"I will, once I get the lights on."

"There's something to be said for fiber-optic trees," she called after him.

"Bah, humbug," he called back, causing her to giggle again.

He was right about the scent of a real tree, though, she thought as she leaned her head back and looked at the corner of her living room where he was installing it. The tree smelled wonderful, carrying her back to happier times, to memories of childhood excitement.

He returned shortly with his coffee and her milk. She held her glass perched on her belly. Like having a handy shelf, she thought wryly. "So," she asked, "did you get excited about Christmas when you were a kid?"

"Believe it." He sat on the edge of the couch, mug in hand, smiling. "There were times I had trouble sleeping, and not only when I was little."

"Me, too," she agreed. "My excitement always started ratcheting with the first snowfall. I could feel magic in the air. I remember when I was fifteen and too excited to sleep, and telling myself that was ridiculous for someone of my age. That was for the little kids. Didn't work."

He chuckled. "I wasn't any better. My sister, however, was a pain. Somehow she slept. Worse, she slept in. I had diabolical ways of waking her up when I got too impatient."

"I had to wait in my bedroom until my folks put on some Christmas music. They always wanted to make coffee before they unleashed me. Mom left a stocking on the door, though."

"You, too? But that stocking didn't tamp my impatience for very long. I used to think there had to be something wrong with my sister. How in the world could she sleep in on Christmas morning? Even when she was young. What five-year-old does that?"

"Your sister?" she suggested.

He laughed. "Apparently so."

She was enjoying seeing this side of him. He looked younger than when he'd arrived, and for the first time, she didn't feel like she was sharing quarters with a cat that was always poised to pounce. Right now he was very comfortable to share space with.

And sexy as hell, she thought with no guilt. As he sat

there in his plain blue flannel shirt and jeans, elbows resting on splayed knees, she felt the sizzle, felt the longing…and he wasn't even doing anything to encourage it. What was it about him? The man in him seemed to call effortlessly to the woman in her.

She remembered the feeling of his arms around her, and admitted that the simple hug had filled an aching hole deep within her. She wanted more hugs, and as she watched him resume hanging the lights, she acknowledged that she wanted a whole lot more than that. She wondered what it would feel like to run her hands over that hard body, to discover his contours. To feel his hands running over her skin, everywhere, touching places that hadn't been touched in so long. She wanted him to fill all her senses until she thought of nothing else.

But as he'd reminded her, they were both sorting things out. Maybe this mood was as ephemeral as everything else. Maybe she didn't deserve stolen moments of happiness, and what if they wrecked her more? Because Ryker would be moving on, back to a dangerous job. The very kind of life she had already lived with Johnny. She didn't think she could do that again.

In fact, she was quite certain. Not with a baby. So, steamy thoughts aside, she needed to avoid anything that could hurt her again. Anything.

When the lights were at last on the Christmas tree, Ryker stood back to eye his handiwork. There were some blotches of color, but not much and not too many. "Okay?" he asked Marisa.

"It's beautiful."

Seeing her smile made it all worthwhile. He would, he realized, do almost anything to keep that smile there.

That expression had been so rare when he had arrived, but now he was glimpsing a new Marisa, one who was no longer totally buried in her grief.

Oh, the grief was still there. He was no fool. She'd spend the rest of her life grieving for John, but the healing hands of time should ease it, lessen it, put it further in the background most of the time. If he could help that along, he would.

"I'm gonna get some more coffee before I start decorating," he said. "Want anything?"

"I need to move around a bit," she said decisively. As she started to wiggle forward, to get her feet properly balanced before she stood, he held out his hands. Without hesitating, she took them, and he tugged her gently up.

"I think I'll keep you," she said lightly. "Getting up is getting harder."

She stood only a few inches from him, and her natural scents filled him. His whole body responded with need. He forced himself to focus on what she'd said. "How come?"

"My balance has changed. It just takes a little more thinking and a little more work now. No biggie."

He looked down into her amazing eyes, saw a smile there. "And how's Jonni doing?"

"She's fine. She's been a little quiet this evening, but still stirring."

"That must be the most amazing experience." Reluctantly, he let go of her hands, reminding himself that there were limits here, wise ones. Limits that protected them both from making a mistake. He didn't want to do anything she would regret, because if he did he'd be living with a pile of regret, too, and he wasn't a man filled with regrets.

He'd made his choices and lived with them. He couldn't see any point in regret because the past couldn't be changed; it could only teach lessons. He had, however, known plenty of people who could devote a whole lot of time to regrets, and he didn't know if Marisa was one of them.

He didn't really know her at all. Nor did she really know him. Worse, his secrets stood between them like an insurmountable barrier. Every time he failed to reveal who John had been working for, he committed another lie by omission. Yeah, he was bound to it, but you couldn't build anything on lies. The whole thing would be rotten, riddled by them. As she walked toward the kitchen, his gaze followed her, and he felt a savage hatred for the secrecy forced on him.

God, he needed to make some changes.

His cell phone rang, surprising him, and he pulled it out. The office, of course. Why the hell were they bothering him?

He grabbed his jacket and called to Marisa. "I'm stepping outside to take this call. Back in a minute."

"Okay," she responded.

Outside, the snow continued to fall. More shoveling in the morning. Making sure no one was within earshot, he answered the call before he even zipped his jacket.

"Tremaine."

It was Bill. He recognized the voice instantly. "You've been rattling some bars, R.T."

"I want to know. And there's a woman who deserves to know."

"Of course she deserves to know. That doesn't change anything. It can't change anything."

"Then at least have someone deliver the letter, let

her know about the star. Someday she might even want to show the star to her child. Is that really too freaking much?"

Bill didn't say anything for a few seconds. "Maybe that's possible. I'll look into it. But stop rattling the cage. Some folks are getting nervous about you."

As if he cared anymore. This had become personal. Maybe that reduced his effectiveness, but to hell with it. The certainty had been growing in him that, given his experience and expertise, he was far more valuable to them than they were to him.

"I'll let you know." Then Bill was gone.

He stuffed his phone into his jeans pocket and stood for a while watching the snow fall. It was beautiful, but tonight it reminded him of frozen tears.

Finally he shook himself, remembering that Marisa was inside, probably wondering what was going on.

He found her in the kitchen, and all the happiness that had been written on her face was gone now. She sat at the table with a glass of cranberry juice and looked hollowly at him. "You have to leave."

It sounded almost like an accusation. "No. Absolutely not. That was just a loose end."

Her hands were wrapped around the glass, her knuckles white. "You don't need to lie to me."

"I'm not lying. I don't have to leave."

"Johnny got calls like that, then he'd be gone."

He blew a loud breath, then said firmly, "I am not John, and I am not lying." Except by all he couldn't say.

Of course he wasn't John. But he was so like John that it made no difference, he supposed. He got his cup of coffee, then sat facing her, tree forgotten. One phone call and her day was destroyed. In that instant he had a clear and ugly picture of what she had endured.

Reaching across the table, he pried her hands from the glass. They were now cold and damp. He swallowed them in his grip, holding on to her. He had a bridge to cross here, and he needed to do it quickly.

"You want the truth?" he asked.

She nodded, her face drooping.

"I've been trying to find out what happened to John."

She caught her breath. "And?"

"And nothing yet. In fact, I got told to let it go. I can't say more than that."

Her expression changed suddenly, her eyes widening a bit, despair replaced by worry. "You're not losing your job over this?"

"No." Flat and firm. "But I guess I made some folks uneasy."

All of a sudden her small hands gripped his back. "Don't do this, Ryker. Don't get yourself in trouble by trying to answer my questions. I'd hate it. I'd hate myself."

"I've pressed it as far as I can," he said honestly. "So don't worry about me. Besides, I think I'm close to shoving this job."

"Really?" Her expression lightened a bit. "But what will you do?"

"If there's one thing I know I can do, it's take care of myself. I'm not worried about it. Now, how about we get back to the tree?"

Marisa helped decorate the tree. Well, the middle section of the tree, she admitted, feeling her mood improve. She couldn't bend over too much, didn't dare squat, and Ryker wouldn't let her reach high for fear she might lose her balance. He was big enough to work over her head, and he clearly had no difficulty squatting.

"This is turning out pretty good," he said halfway through. "Did I buy enough ornaments?"

She eyed the tree and the remaining boxes. "More than enough," she assured him. "If we use them all, we won't be able to see much of the tree."

He laughed. "Can't have that. You like blue spruce."

He was squatting beside her, and as she reached to the side to hang another bauble, she teetered a bit and quickly grabbed his shoulder for balance. Muscle stirred beneath her hand, and heat stirred between her thighs.

"You'd better take a break," he said. "You don't want an early Christmas present."

So she returned to her chair to watch as he finished up. So many bright colors, and the LED lights sparkled everywhere. He'd spared nothing on this project.

But he didn't seem like a man for half measures. Why would she be surprised by that? Johnny hadn't been one, either. The similarity at once disturbed her and comforted her.

If there was one thing she'd learned about men like Johnny and Ryker, it was that they did what they said they'd do, with full commitment. She liked that.

"There," he said finally, stepping back. "What do you think? I don't want to bury it."

She studied it, the smile coming back to her face. "It's beautiful. I love it."

He grinned at her, started to gather up boxes and un- used ornaments, then paused. "How about lights out- side? Do you want me to do them?"

Amazement filled her, then humor, which unleashed

a laugh. "Are you crazy, Ryker? It's cold out there, and that would be a whole lot of work and expense."

"True," he agreed, settling across from her. "On the other hand, I haven't decorated the outside of a house since I was a kid."

"Oh. I never did…before. I like looking at other people's houses, but I've never done it." He'd missed a lot, she thought, and she didn't want to deprive him of this if he wanted it.

"Well, we don't have to. It crossed my mind."

Why was she raising objections? The Christmas tree delighted her, had brought a breath of fresh air into this house, one she had needed. Because of a Christmas tree, she had enjoyed nearly the entire day. Was that so wrong?

Then she understood something else. "Would you decorate outside because you want it, or because you think I'd want it?"

"Both, actually. I was thinking about how pretty it would be, and how I haven't done it in so long. But it's up to you." He glanced at his watch. "Maude's is still open. Want some hot chocolate? People have been raving about it. Apparently she's spiced it up a bit with cinnamon."

She wondered if he was having trouble holding still. "I'd like that," she said finally.

"I'll be right back, then. In the meantime, you think about outside decorations."

Maybe that call from work had bothered him, she thought as he went out the door. Certainly he hadn't seemed quite as lighthearted since then. But he could just be tired, too. He'd been out in the cold an awful lot today, going for the tree, cutting it before bringing it inside, then running to the store for all those ornaments…

Or maybe she was looking for benign explanations where there were none. She had a habit of doing that.

He said he wasn't in any trouble for trying to find out more about Johnny's death, but he might just have said that so she wouldn't worry. She didn't want him to have problems because of her. But would he admit it if he were?

Probably not. He seemed hell-bent on protecting her. Her friends had been trying to care for her all along, and she'd kept a distance, denying them the right to do something that would probably make them feel good. But then this man Ryker came out of nowhere, and somehow he'd worked his way past her resistance. She seemed more aware of what he might need as Johnny's friend than she had been aware of what *her* friends might need.

Gloom settled over her as she contemplated the selfishness that grief had created in her. She had some serious making up to do.

Ryker returned quickly with the hot chocolate and put a foam cup on the table beside her. "I picked up a couple of crullers, too. Want one?"

"I'd love it." At least he looked as if his troubles had fled while he was out. She leaned her head back, staring at the beautiful tree they'd made together, thinking she needed to apologize seriously to some friends. Maybe have them over for a little Christmas party. Let them know how much she loved them.

"Outside decorations?" he asked as he settled himself with his own cocoa and cruller.

She thought about how it would brighten up the place, how it would welcome her friends if she gave a small party. "If you really want to do it," she said. "And I was thinking about having a small get-together with some friends. I've been pretty much leaving them out in the cold for a long time now. Would you mind?"

"You're asking *me*? Your house, Marisa."

"I'm still asking."

He shook his head a little, then smiled. "Party away. Won't trouble me at all. But let me get the stuff outside up first."

A smile surprised her, tipping up the corners of her mouth. "It would certainly look like an invitation."

One she hadn't issued in forever, it seemed like.

He turned off all the lights except for the tree, and she sat in its magical glow, feeling everything inside her beginning to shift, as if something elemental had changed. Almost without knowing it, she had reached a decision.

At last she rose from the rocker and walked over to him, standing right in front of him. He looked up at her and put aside his own cup.

"Ryker." Her heart beat so fast she wondered if she would collapse.

"Yes?"

"Take me to bed, please."

A hundred emotions seemed to run over the face she had once thought looked like granite. "Are you sure?"

She nodded. She was sure of one thing: she was awakening, and she wanted to complete her awakening wrapped in Ryker's arms.

Chapter Nine

For Ryker, sex had always been easy to come by, easy to enjoy, casual and meaningless. As he rose and took Marisa's hand, he knew this was different. Very different. First there was her pregnancy. Then there was this woman's ability to shake him to his very core. This would be no casual encounter, but rather one that could change everything.

In his life he'd taken a lot of risks, but suddenly none of them seemed as huge as this. Worse, looking into her face he understood to his very core that turning her down would inflict a wound. She had taken a bold step, reaching for life again, but he suspected she didn't feel especially attractive right now, and he hadn't spent any effort on trying to make her understand that she was attractive to him in ways no other woman had been. He'd been avoiding all the build-up to this moment because he didn't want to harm her. With one word, right now when she was so vulnerable, he could have gutted her.

She had taken the decision right out of his hands.

He spoke quietly. "You *did* talk to your doctor?"

She nodded, her gaze hopeful and even a little frightened.

"That must have knocked him sideways under the circumstances."

He was relieved to see a slight smile dance around her mouth. "If it did, he didn't show it."

"Restrictions?"

"I have to lie on my side. Ryker…"

He could see it. She thought he was looking for a way out. That pierced him painfully, and he wasted no more time. For whatever reason, she needed this, and he wanted it. "Well," he said forcing a smile of his own, "there are plenty of ways to give pleasure."

Relief filled him as he saw her relax a bit. One thorny hill surmounted. All of a sudden, though, he became aware of his own inadequacies. He'd never made love to a pregnant woman. He had no idea how this would roll. No mission plan other than giving her a wonderful experience. A daunting task under these conditions. He wondered if he'd be good enough, careful enough, considerate enough…

And all the while he was wondering, he was leading her to her bedroom. The prepared baby crib at the foot of her bed seemed to glow with warning. A dangerous situation.

But it didn't dampen his desire for her. That had been plaguing him, and like a smoldering fire it had refused to go out. Now those embers were glowing, beginning to heat him throughout. He couldn't let them take control.

If ever his self-control had been tested, this would be one of the rare times he wasn't certain he had enough. Inside him flames were leaping. His body was already burgeoning and throbbing. Marisa became the sole focus of his universe.

He left the lamp on because he wanted to see her. He slipped his arms around her as they stood beside her bed, trying to support her back, and leaned in for their first kiss.

To have come to this point without any kisses, without any touches… A dance like this usually had some lead-in time, but not this time. It had arrived with a bang, like a herd of thundering horses. Everything he'd been avoiding, everything that should have preceded these moments, was missing, and he had to make it up to her.

Her mouth tasted sweet, of chocolate and cruller, but her tongue showed no shyness. He felt her hands grip his shoulders as their tongues dueled, as he swept the inside of her mouth and felt a shiver run through her. Her lips clung to his, drinking from him, speaking in a way no words ever could.

He could have lost himself right then and there, but he couldn't forget her precious cargo or her back. He didn't want her to start hurting, to lose these moments with a backache or other discomfort.

Tearing his mouth from hers, he took a half step back to reach for the hem of the shirt she wore. Johnny's shirt, he was sure. For an instant he wondered if he was betraying his friend, then dismissed the notion. Johnny was gone. He and Marisa were here.

No buttons fought him. He pulled the shirt away and filled his gaze with the sight of her full breasts, cased in white cotton, and the smooth bulge of her belly just below them.

Bending, he kissed her belly. "I'll take it easy."

Marisa's hands cradled his head, holding him close as he rested his cheek on her belly. She caressed his hair, making him feel utterly welcome. Still kissing her tummy, he hooked his thumbs in the waistband of her pants and panties and pulled them down.

A gasp escaped her, further enflaming him. God, he wanted this. When he got her pants to her knees, he urged her to sit.

"I want to look at you," he murmured. "But first we have to get rid of some stuff."

A breathless laugh escaped her as she settled on the edge of the bed. Getting rid of her pants and slippers was easy. Then, kneeling in front of her, he pulled her head to his shoulder and reached for the clasp of her bra. As he released it, she drew a sharp breath. "Ryker..."

"I know," he said, as his entire body pulsed. "I know." If she was feeling anything like he was, they were going to light the night with their explosion.

Leaning back, he took her in. Her breasts were full, looking so firm as they readied for the child. Her areolae were slightly brown, unexpected, given her coloring. The secret place between her thighs was partly hidden. He'd never seen a more perfect picture.

Rising, he shed his own clothes quickly. "Condom?" he asked gruffly, wanting to be done with the last necessity.

"Bedside table," she whispered.

He found the drawer and put the box on top of the table, beside the bed. Then he faced the woman he wanted with every cell of his being.

He realized she was sweeping him with a hungry gaze, taking in every detail. She could no longer miss how much he wanted her. But she also had to see the scars, and he hoped they didn't turn her off.

"Ryker," she murmured, "you're beautiful."

"That's my line," he said. "You're the beautiful one. Stand up?"

The moment and passion had gripped her, he realized. She stood boldly, letting him see her delightful curves, unashamed of her swollen belly. That delighted him, but with so much passion hammering him now, he tucked away the memory for later.

He reached out to cup her heavy breasts, feeling how firm they were, brushing his thumbs over her engorged nipples. As he did so, she gasped.

"Hurts?" he asked, concern pushing hunger briefly aside.

"No, oh, no," she said faintly. "Feels too good, so good…"

The image of her seared his mind. He knew he would never forget this moment, this gift. Then she lowered herself to the bed, stretching out, giving him another gift of her complete trust.

Something was being born in him, but he didn't want to think about that now. A beautiful woman was offering herself to him, a priceless offering. It touched him and stoked the blaze inside him, and he knew he would never be the same.

Carefully he stretched out beside her and, propped on one elbow, he began to explore her with his hand, stroking downward over every hill and curve. She responded to each touch as if it was electric. He dropped more kisses on her, sparing not an inch of her. She kept reaching for him, but with the last remnants of reason he remembered he must be careful. Supremely careful.

When at last he put his mouth to her breast and sucked, she arched and groaned and her fingers clawed at him, trying to drag him closer. Hammered by his own need, it was almost impossible for him to resist. Had he ever ached so hard for any woman?

His body wanted to take over, but he couldn't let it. The baby. He kept reminding himself, the last sane thought in a world spinning rapidly out of control. In near desperation, he urged her onto her side so that he lay behind her. His hand made another trip over her, causing her to cry out with pleasure, finding her breasts exquisitely sensitive, so sensitive that she finally clasped her hand to hold it there.

"Never stop," she begged, sounding as desperate as he felt.

But he had other plans in mind. Pulling his hand free, he dragged it lower until at last he found the dewy place between her thighs. He slipped his own leg between hers, separating her, opening her to his touch.

The instant his finger found her sensitive nub of nerves, a deep groan escaped her. She reached back with one hand, seeking to hang on to him while he stroked her repeatedly and listened to her breathing grow more and more ragged. Her nails found his buttocks and dug in, driving him crazy with renewed hunger. He refused to give in. First her. He wanted to bring her to completion before anything else, to show her that he could give her everything while taking little for himself. He needed to give her that.

She rocked gently against his touches, her cries coming more often. He kissed the nape of her neck, savoring each movement she took toward satisfaction. He could feel her electric response inside himself as if they were wired together.

Then, finally, one great spasm took her. A beautiful cry escaped her. Satisfied, he cupped her with his hand, pressing hard, drawing the last drop out for her.

Her ears almost felt as if they rang from the intensity of her orgasm. Ryker had given her a wholly new experience, and as she slowly drifted back to earth, she listened to them both breathe raggedly. Gradually she came back, feeling the cool air of the room on her heated skin, feeling the man behind her keeping her warm with his own body heat. Holding her so gently and intimately. Feeling his erection hard against her bottom.

"Ryker?" she whispered.

"How are you?"

"Wonderful. Fantastic. But what about you?"

"Don't worry about it."

She stirred, grabbing his hand, bringing it to her lips, smelling herself on him. A new arc of desire passed through her. "Please," she murmured. "I want... Fill me. I need it."

For long seconds he didn't reply. Maybe he couldn't figure out how to do this. She didn't really know herself. She just knew that a part of her had been empty for too long, and she needed a man to fill it. This man. Not just anyone, but Ryker. She didn't question the need, she just accepted it.

"Just a sec," he said finally. He pulled away. She heard him open a condom, and her heart began to race again. When he came back, he slipped his leg between hers again and started caressing her from breast to belly. Never in her life had her breasts been so exquisitely sensitive. Something else good to say about pregnancy, she thought distantly as desire began to sizzle through her with renewed power.

"Promise me," he murmured as he kissed her neck and caressed her breasts, "you'll tell me if anything hurts even a tiny bit."

"Promise," she answered with the last bit of air she seemed to be able to find. She was flying again, rising to the heights with this man. His hand found her center and the knot of exquisite nerves. For just an instant his touch almost hurt, but then her body began the inevitable blossoming.

"Ryker?" Impatience began to drive her.

"Shh…" A mere whisper as his fingers lashed her back to the precipice. Then, she felt him enter her, stretching her, filling her, answering a need she had forgotten she had. It felt so good to be filled with him, so good.

Then he drove her crazy by continuing to caress her and move very slowly within her. Gently. He didn't look like a gentle man, but his tenderness with her was amazing.

Little by little he carried her up, refusing to increase his pace, making her want to cry out for more. But he didn't give it to her, drawing the experience out, taking half a lifetime in which she reached new pinnacles of longing and pleasure, until the ache became too much to bear. Then, at last, the explosion rolled over her, leaving her nearly blind with its intensity. Only dimly did she feel him stiffen behind her, followed by the throbbing of his member as he reached his own satisfaction.

Replete, exhausted, she tumbled with him into utter bliss.

* * *

She fell asleep almost instantly. That amused Ryker, but he figured she'd had a long day, and she hadn't taken her usual nap. He reached across the bed, trying not to disturb her, and managed to pull most of the blankets over her to keep her warm.

Then he lay holding her, staring at the wall beyond her bed, dealing with the sense that something inside him had just changed permanently. No other sexual experience had left him feeling that way, except his very first, but Marisa had somehow changed him.

Or maybe the change had been coming on for a while. He'd certainly begun questioning himself in ways he never had before. Deep inside him resided an uncomfortable feeling, the sense that he was unworthy to hold this woman.

She didn't make him feel that way, but the very fact that he was feeling it acted like a warning flag. At some level he was trying to deal with a basic fact: he could go back to his regular life, or he could make a drastic change so he wouldn't feel unworthy of the gift Marisa had just given him.

He needed to be wary of such questions because they could blunt his edge, and all too often his life depended on his edge. So, pretty soon here he was going to have to answer the question: Was he going back or taking a different direction?

His hand rested over her belly, atop the blanket, and he felt the baby stir and kick. Absolutely magical. He spread his hand so he could feel it better and thought about a new little girl coming into this world, all shiny and spotless and eager for life. He'd like to feel even a touch of that eagerness again. He supposed Marisa would, too.

Life left no one shiny and spotless, though. Everyone got dinged and picked up some stains. Life sometimes shoveled manure as if it were a game.

The question was what you did about it. He thought he'd been accomplishing good and important things, that the inevitable stains didn't outweigh the good he'd done. Then he thought about a fatherless child who would soon enter this world and wondered whether any of his past missions could ever outweigh the importance of caring for a child.

Maybe Johnny had missed his boat to redemption.

Ryker sighed quietly and tried to wipe the questions from his head. He had grown increasingly certain that he needed to change something, that he was getting tired of his mission-oriented life, but he had to be careful about what he chose.

His parents kept nagging him to settle down, especially his mother. Sometimes he was quite certain that she believed he was a changeling. They didn't know any more about what he did than Marisa, but they knew it wasn't "normal." His mother's worried gaze popped up in his mind's eye, and he felt her concern for him reach across the miles. He could never answer her questions, nor erase her fears for him, not as long as he kept his job. His missions were important, but maybe he'd failed to consider how they affected others. The way John had apparently never given any real thought to what might become of Marisa.

On the one hand he was making sacrifices for his country. On the other he was stealing something from the people he cared about most. Facing that, he knew the time for change had come. No ifs, ands or buts. The attitude shift in him answered the question.

Now all he had to do was figure it out.

Marisa slept through the entire night. When her eyes popped open and saw the digital clock beside the bed, she started. She was alone in the bed, and now she was embarrassed. What a way to treat Ryker after their incredible lovemaking. Hurrying, she popped out of bed, showered and dressed quickly in one of Johnny's old sweatshirts and a pair of stretchy fleece pants.

She found Ryker in the kitchen enjoying coffee with a stack of toast on the table. He looked at her with a warm smile. "Sleep well?" he asked.

"I can't believe… Ryker, I'm sorry. That was rude."

"Rude?" He shook his head, laughing quietly, and rose to wrap her in his arms. She leaned into him, loving the way it felt to be held by him. Then, gently, he turned her around so that she leaned back into his embrace. One of his hands settled over her swollen belly, the other cupped her breast boldly, causing her to gasp with instant pleasure.

"No apologies," he said, dropping a kiss on her neck. "It was wonderful. You were tired. How are you and how's your little passenger?"

"We're fine. We're better than fine," she admitted, relaxing into him. "It was so beautiful."

"It was," he agreed, his voice nearly a deep purr. "Perfect. But now I need to feed you."

She felt reluctance as he released her and urged her into a chair. As she sat, she realized she didn't want him to let go of her. She wanted him to take her back to bed and bring that miraculous magic to her once more.

Just looking at him made her ache with hunger. She no longer cared why it had happened; it had just happened, and right now it made her feel happy. She was allowed that, right?

He fed her scrambled eggs and toast, along with a cup of coffee and a tall glass of orange juice. He sat across from her with his own coffee, just smiling.

There was a peace to this morning, the kind of peace she hadn't felt in a long time. For once she didn't even remind herself that he'd leave her the way Johnny had so often. This morning none of that mattered.

Her appetite seemed to have reawakened with her, and she ate heartily…at least until shyness began to overtake her. She wasn't usually a shy person, but so much had changed last night. The intimacy they'd shared… All of a sudden, the memory of how she had cut loose, how she had asked Ryker to take her to bed, overwhelmed her. How did they move forward now? She didn't have a thing to say, even though her body was still vibrating at his presence.

"Marisa? Are you regretting last night?"

She glanced up and saw that his face had shadowed, lost some of its relaxation. "No," she said swiftly. "I'm just…it's just…" She bit her lip. "I don't know where we go from here. I just feel…shy, I guess. Unsure. Last night changed things, and I don't know quite what to say or do."

She darted a look at him and was amazed to see him smiling. "Ah," he said as if he understood that garble.

"Ah?"

He tilted his head to one side briefly, a kind of shrug. "I think I get it. Well, this doesn't change anything you don't want it to change. I'm still the same Ryker, except that I happen to be feeling quite special this morning."

"You feel special?" The idea amazed her.

He nodded and leaned forward, reaching for her hand. "You gave me an incredible gift. Why wouldn't I feel special?"

"But...you gave me something special, too."

"I hope so. Just relax and be yourself. I wouldn't change one hair on your head, Marisa Hayes. Not one. You're beautiful, you're generous with yourself, you're a loving person. You deserve every good thing in life. If I gave you one of them, then I'm a very lucky guy."

Wow, that was overwhelming from a man who had often seemed to her to live behind impenetrable walls. Except those walls had been coming down, like with the Christmas tree yesterday. For whatever reason, he was reaching out for something. Maybe not her, but he was reaching, and she suspected he was trying to regain something he'd lost.

She turned her hand over, clasping his in return. "Thank you."

His smile deepened. "Today's a good day for just basking in the glow, don't you think?"

"Carpe diem?" she asked.

He laughed. "I take 'em where I can get 'em."

Which reminded her of when he had said that he *loved 'em and left 'em*. He'd warned her, and she'd reached for him, anyway. But certainly she wasn't naive enough to fall for him. She knew their time together was limited. No, she wasn't foolish enough to do that.

So why not just enjoy the day?

They cuddled on the couch much of the day, taking time to eat, enjoying the tree and desultory conversation that just kind of rambled. It wasn't as if either of them were in a mood to dive into deep emotional waters.

Hardly surprising her, he admitted to having been a bit of a daredevil as a kid and showed her the scars to prove it. Stitches and broken bones had been common for him as a child, and he recounted the time his mother had stood beside him in the emergency room and just burst out with, "Will you, please, just live long enough to grow up?"

"I think I was hard on her," he admitted. "She tried to shrug a lot of it off as natural high jinks, but finally it really started to get to her. I behaved a little better after that."

"Really? I'm supposed to believe that?"

"Well, there were only a few more stitches and no broken bones."

She sighed, feeling his shoulder beneath the back of her head. His arm wrapped around her, beneath her breasts and just over her belly. She spoke. "I think I'm glad I'm having a girl."

"Nothing says a girl can't be a daredevil, too."

She laughed. "I guess not."

"What about you?"

"Nothing like you. I was kind of a geek or a nerd, or whatever it's called these days. Always buried in books. Part of the chess team and debate team. Editor of the school paper. A bookworm, in short."

"You're one helluva pretty bookworm."

"I didn't date," she admitted. "I'm not sure, but I think I scared guys off."

"I can't imagine it."

"Well, I sure didn't appeal to them."

He lifted his hand, cupping her breast. "Say that one more time, I dare you."

"What are you going to do?" she demanded.

"This?" He rubbed his palm back and forth across the peak of her breast. She wasn't wearing a bra, and her nipple hardened instantly. Shivers of longing poured through her. "Ryker..." she gasped.

"Let me tease you. I think we need to be careful." He stopped caressing her and instead gave her a gentle squeeze.

"My doctor said..."

"I'm sure your doctor was right. But I'm not sure he was imagining a marathon. For your sake, I can wait. How about you?"

She sighed, closing her eyes, clamping her thighs together to quiet her hunger. "I suppose you're right."

"Maybe better than finding out someone was totally wrong."

She couldn't deny it.

"Besides, I'm really enjoying this, holding you like this. Sad truth about Ryker Tremaine?"

"Sure."

"I don't do this. Ever. But here I am, and I'm thinking about all I chose to miss until you came along."

Her heart filled with an odd combination of pleasure and pain. Pleased that he was content with holding her like this, sad that he had missed so much. "That was sweet," she said.

"Just the unvarnished truth. Any other time in my life I wouldn't have been here this morning."

She caught her breath. The swelling in her heart no longer contained any pleasure at all. She couldn't tell which of them she hurt more for, him or her. This was ephemeral, she reminded herself. A passing moment he might well forget as soon as he left. Meaningless. It had to be meaningless, because she couldn't return to the life she had lived with Johnny. Not now. Not with a baby.

"Anyway," he said presently, "don't you have a party to plan? We could talk about that. And about whether to do the front of the house and how much decorating we should do."

"You want to go to the store?"

His arm tightened a bit around her midsection. "Not today. I don't want to lose one second with you."

Warmth flooded her, banishing the phantoms of fear that had started to hover nearby again. Take it for what it was. Enjoy the day.

For the first time since the funeral she honestly believed that the future was worth living for. She was alive again, and regardless of what loomed, she didn't want to lose a second with Ryker, either.

Chapter Ten

"Good morning."

She awoke to feel Ryker's breath on her neck, along with a peppering of light kisses. He'd made love to her again during the night, gentle yet explosive love, and she felt cherished to her very soul.

"'Morning," she said sleepily, stirring happily to his touches. She was tangled in the blankets, and when she tried to turn over to face him, he had to help her. He was smiling.

She felt herself smile in response, felt her heart lift. A surprisingly tender man, one she hadn't thought he could be when she first met him. Ryker had exposed a whole side of himself to her that she would have bet he rarely shared.

"How's the passenger?" he asked.

"She's fine." A poke answered her, as if the baby was saying good morning, as well.

"I'm still in awe," he admitted. First he ran his hand over her belly, then swept it down her back, pressing her bottom to bring her closer. "You are irresistible," he murmured before stealing a long, deep kiss.

When she could breathe again, she asked, "Even with bed head?"

"Especially with bed head." He flashed her a grin. "Should I make breakfast?"

"I could do it," she offered.

"I know you could. But I like to feel helpful."

"What do you call last night?"

That drew a belly laugh from him. He stole another quick kiss, then rolled out of bed in all his naked glory. She lay there smiling into her pillow as he took a quick shower, then headed for the kitchen in jeans and a T-shirt.

Her turn now, she supposed, but she hated to leave the bed just yet. She could still feel his warmth, could still detect his scent and the scent of last night's lovemaking.

She closed her eyes and let Johnny's memory surface. She hoped he wouldn't be upset with her but could no longer imagine why he should be. Julie had been right. He'd been the one who kept leaving. And finally he had left for good.

Sighing, she at last pulled herself up and into the shower. Everywhere she rubbed herself with soap and a washcloth, she found herself remembering Ryker's hands on her.

She realized as she toweled off that he had wedged himself into her life, and that when he left, the sorrow was now inevitable. She'd miss him. But she would survive.

For the first time, she appreciated the fact that while

she had withdrawn from life for so long in her grief, she had gotten through the worst of it. She was strong. Selfish in some ways, but strong in the important ways.

Strong enough to be left again. Strong enough to raise her baby. Strong.

She and Ryker were just finishing breakfast when Julie bounced in through the side door. She grinned at both of them, bringing a blast of frigid air in with her before she shoved the door closed.

"My, don't you two look cozy," she remarked cheerfully, shedding her scarf and jacket. "How's it going?"

Then she peered at Marisa and shot a sharp look at Ryker.

"My, my," she said.

Marisa felt her cheeks heat. "Cut it out, Julie."

"Why?" Julie headed for the coffeepot, filled a mug and came to sit with them. "You look more relaxed than I've seen you in forever. Your face doesn't look pinched."

Marisa didn't know how to respond to that. All she knew was that she didn't want to discuss with Julie what had happened. It was private, a secret to keep to herself and savor.

"Vast improvement," Julie went on. "It had better stay that way. So how are you feeling, other than relaxed?"

"I'm fine," Marisa answered promptly. Better than fine, but there was no point saying anything that would only draw out more questions. "I was thinking of having a party for my friends. I've been so withdrawn, and I think I owe you guys all an apology."

Julie became instantly diverted. She waved a hand. "You don't owe any apologies. But a party in your state? What kind of party?"

"Something simple."

Julie flashed another grin. "I could manage it for you."

Marisa shook her head. "If you throw the party, how am I thanking all my friends for sticking with me? No, I'll just do something simple. Coffee and Christmas cookies. I just want to let everyone know I still love them. They must have wondered."

Julie reached for her hand and gave it a quick squeeze. "Everyone understood, hon. And what kind of friends would we be if we didn't stick beside you? It'll do us all some good to see you start taking steps out of hibernation. That's all we need."

She sniffed the air. "Do I smell pine?"

"Ryker put up a Christmas tree."

Julie turned her attention on him. "For real? A real tree?"

He smiled and nodded.

Julie grinned hugely. "Fantastic! The last few years Marisa didn't even bother to put up that fiber-optic tree of hers. As if it was too much trouble when Johnny wouldn't be home. Now, that was sad."

Marisa watched something pass between the two of them. What was it? A warning? An understanding?

"Well, this I've got to see," Julie announced, bouncing up out of her chair and carrying her coffee to the living room.

Marisa looked at Ryker almost apologetically, but he simply smiled and shrugged. Well, if he wasn't disturbed by this intrusion, she certainly wasn't. Julie had a habit of popping in at odd times, and ordinarily Marisa was glad to see her. It was just that this time…this time, what? She wanted to be alone with Ryker? Foolish hope.

They followed Julie into the living room, and Ryker turned on the lights for her.

"Awesome!" was Julie's pronouncement. "And you finally got your blue spruce. I love it!"

"Well," she said, turning to Marisa, "a gang of over-hyper five-year-olds awaits me. Christmas turns them into demons, I swear. I envy their anticipation and excitement, but controlling it is a job for a whole army."

She gave Marisa a hug, set her coffee cup in the sink and vanished through the door.

"Is she always such a whirlwind?" Ryker asked, sounding almost bemused.

"No, but sometimes. I think she's worrying about me."

"She doesn't have anything to worry about," he said with a firmness that surprised her.

Now what the hell did that mean?

But Ryker had returned to sphinx mode and left her wondering.

Three days later, Ryker was out in the cold hanging the lights Marisa had agreed to, along with a wreath for the front door. The day was bitter, and he ducked inside often for a cup of coffee and a few minutes to warm up. Marisa was calling her friends, inviting them over for coffee and cookies. As he watched her chat with them, smiling and looking content, he knew he was in trouble.

He needed to start pulling away. She was showing signs of caring for him, like the way she always had hot coffee ready for him when he came inside. Other little things were mounting up, too.

Nobody had ever cared for him this way, and it worried him. But every time he told himself to start forging some space between them, he discovered something that troubled him even more: he couldn't make himself do it.

As he stood on the ladder outside, receiving occasional help and advice from friendly neighbors, he took a long, hard look at himself. He had a weakness, a serious weakness, for Marisa Hayes, and the self-control that had marked his entire adult life vanished the instant he got close to her.

Weakness of any kind was a dangerous thing, for himself and others. He hadn't missed Julie's significant look of warning the other morning. He was determined to heed it but kept failing. Apparently the only way he could separate himself from this woman was to leave, and he refused to do that until after the baby was safely born.

Only then would he feel he'd kept his promise to John.

But as for paying his penance...hell, this all felt too good to be penance. All of it, from standing at the foot of the ladder and talking to the guy next door, to going inside and seeing Marisa's happy face.

He just hoped she wasn't still worried about betraying John. Too bad she'd probably be the one who felt betrayed after he left. Damn, he should never have given in to her, should never have taken her to bed, even though he'd known how his refusal would wound her.

Talk about a rock and a hard place.

He was standing at the foot of the ladder, the job nearly done, when Ray from next door came over for the second time. "It's nice to see Marisa decorating," he remarked. "Fiona likes it. So, you were Johnny's friend, huh?"

Some friend, thought Ryker. "Yeah."

"Good of you to come see her through this. I wonder

if Johnny would have been here? He almost never was."
Then Ray shook his head. "Not my business, especially
not now. Fiona would kill me for mentioning it."

Fiona would kill him? The thought amused Ryker,
since he had gathered that Marisa thought Fiona was a
huge gossip.

Just then two kids tumbled out of the house next door,
laughing and shrieking. School was out for the day. The
holiday vacation began next week, he gathered.

"My call," said Ray. "Time to take them to the skat-
ing rink. See you around."

Ryker watching Ray round up excited children and
pile them into the car. The sight both amused him and
appealed to him. Maybe there were some complications
in being a father, like kids who wanted to play tag when
they needed to be getting into the car.

When the car was gone, Ryker stepped back to sur-
vey his handiwork. It looked okay, actually. Spaced well,
nothing hanging loose. Pleased, he took the ladder to the
detached garage, then went in the side door.

When he entered the kitchen, he knew immediately
that something had changed. Shucking his outerwear,
he dumped it over the kitchen chair and went hunting.
He found Marisa standing in the living room, staring
at the tree.

"Marisa?"

She didn't answer immediately. Concerned, he walked
up behind her and put his hands on her shoulders.

"What's wrong?" he asked.

"Phone call," she said in a thick voice.

"What?" An extremely rare sense of panic began to
fill him. "Did something bad happen?"

"I don't know. Maybe. Probably not." She shook herself a little, but he didn't let go of her. "A man from the State Department is coming to see me on Saturday. He has a letter for me."

Ryker felt gut-punched. He'd gotten it for her, but he hadn't expected it. He knew exactly what she was going to receive, and it didn't offer much information that she didn't already have. When it was over...when it was over, she was going to know the extent of his duplicity.

He cleared his throat. "That's the day of your party. Maybe you should postpone it."

"I tried to postpone him, but I couldn't." She turned, facing him. "Is it a letter from Johnny?" she asked, whispering.

"If they had something like that, you'd have gotten it with the rest of his belongings."

"So, this official?" Her eyes seemed to have sunken, and she wrapped her arms around herself. "More information?"

"I doubt there'll be much." Just the most damning information of all...for him.

She placed a hand over her mouth, closing her eyes, swaying a bit until he steadied her. "I guess you rattled those bars pretty good," she said weakly, then pulled away from him and went back to the kitchen.

Standing alone in the living room, he hated himself. She'd wanted to know, he'd believed she deserved to know, but at that point he hadn't considered all the possible ramifications. She was about to be wounded anew, and he might as well pack his bags and head back to the motel. After this she'd never be able to trust him.

But he couldn't leave her alone with this. Time for his atonement. All the lies he lived were about to come back to haunt him. He was going to pay big-time.

But he deserved it. He absolutely deserved it.

When he finally went out to the kitchen again, Marisa was back on the phone, telling all her friends that something had come up and she needed to postpone the party. Promising to reschedule.

But what he heard in her voice was the rending grief he'd heard when he first arrived. The escape from reality was over.

They were both about to revisit hell.

Marisa felt the change in Ryker from the instant she told him about the call. He knew what was coming, but wasn't about to tell her. Damn these men and their secrets.

Anger bubbled quietly in her as she thought about all the years lost to secrets. All the things that she would never know about her husband, about Ryker. And whatever was coming on Saturday, Ryker clearly felt it could be a problem.

She hated secrets, most especially operational secrets. She half expected that what would come on Saturday was another pile of secrets, this time secrets that *she* would have to keep. God, she hated it. She wanted it over. She wanted the life she had just been starting to rebuild.

Now some guy from State was going to come and destroy it all one way or another. Yes, she wanted to know more about what had happened to Johnny, but she'd begun to make peace with never knowing. Now they were going to sweep that away, and she'd have to start all over again.

She'd begged for this, and Ryker had tried to give it

to her, and now she was wishing she hadn't asked and he hadn't tried.

That wasn't fair to him. She knew it. But even as he was keeping his distance, she realized she was doing the same. They went to bed together at night, but no more lovemaking. She accepted him holding her, and yet she couldn't let him any closer than that.

He seemed to feel the same. He didn't even try. She wanted to badger him, hoping for something to prepare her, but she could feel he would offer no answers. None. Maybe he didn't have them. Maybe he was just giving her space because he knew this was going to reawaken her grief.

How could it not?

Saturday dragged toward them on leaden feet. Hours seemed to stretch endlessly. It seemed now that two strangers lived in this house, the way it had been when he'd first arrived. She hated it, but she skirted anything personal as assiduously as he did.

God, she just wished Saturday would get here so she could deal with whatever it was. It might not be half as bad as she imagined, but from the way Ryker was acting, she doubted it. He knew something—damn him. Didn't he at least owe it to her to prepare her?

She'd have felt a whole lot better if he'd acted as if this visit were a meaningless formality. Instead, she couldn't escape the sense that he knew something bad was on the way. Sometimes she could have hated him. He was part of the secrecy that had taken such a toll on her life. She'd accepted that once, but she refused to accept it again.

Truth. God, she needed truth in her life.

Maybe that was what was coming on Saturday. Truth. But even as she quailed and railed internally, she kept remembering making love with that man. That had been honest. Maybe the only truthful thing about him. Little enough.

When Saturday arrived, she pulled on the only maternity dress she had bothered to buy, a simple dark blue with white piping at the neck. For the first time in countless months she used makeup. She didn't know what this guy from State was expecting, but he wasn't going to find a washed-out hag…even if she felt like one.

"I should be here," Ryker said as she emerged from the bedroom. "I can stay out of the way if you want, but in case…"

"In case what? I already got the worst news."

The bite of her own voice shocked her, and she watched Ryker's face shutter. He might have pulled into himself, but she was driving him away.

She drew a long breath, but she wasn't about to apologize. "Keep your secrets," she added bitterly, then marched into the living room and sat waiting.

"I'll get the door," he said, remaining in the foyer.

"Fine."

Why did she feel as if her life was about to end again? She was probably making too much of this, being unfair. But as she sat with her fists clenched, her baby stirring in her belly, she was through with making excuses for herself or anyone else.

The doorbell rang, and she stiffened. She heard Ryker answer it. It even sounded as if they were exchanging credentials.

Moments later a man in a dark suit entered the living room, carrying a slender portfolio. Behind him she could see Ryker hanging his overcoat on the hall tree.

"Mrs. Hayes?"

"Ms."

"I'm sorry. Ms. Hayes, I'm Dan Crandall. May I sit?"

She waved him to the couch. He sat facing her. Ryker remained standing in the doorway.

"First, I need to lay some groundwork. You were married to John Kenneth Hayes?"

"Yes."

Crandall nodded. "All right. I'm going to show you a letter and a couple of photographs. They're classified, so I won't be able to leave them with you. Do you understand?"

"Oh, I understand secrecy," she said, reaching for pleasant and barely succeeding.

Crandall gave a fleeting smile. "I imagine you do. I also have to tell you that you won't be able to discuss this information with anyone. Your child can eventually know, but no one else. This information could endanger the lives of others."

For the first time she understood that there was more involved here than her own loss. She nodded, her mouth turning dry.

"All right." He opened his portfolio and passed her a photograph of a wall with black stars on it. "See the star circled in red? That's your husband's. His name will never appear on it."

She swallowed hard, staring at it.

"In front of the wall in that case you see is a carefully guarded book with all the names of our fallen agents inscribed. The public can't look. The only time families can is during our annual memorial service. Henceforth, you will be invited to attend. It's up to you whether you come or not."

She drew a long breath, nodding as he took the photo back.

"This," he said, handing her another, "is a photo of your husband's inscription in the book. I'm sorry we had to black out the other names, but I'm sure you understand."

She wasn't sure she understood any of this. Stars without names? A book no one could see? But staring down at Johnny's carefully inscribed name, she felt the pain pierce her all over again. At least others would never forget him or forget his sacrifice.

When he took that photo back, he offered her a sheet of paper. As soon as she saw the letterhead, her world turned black.

When she came to, she was lying on her back with a worried Ryker over her.

"Marisa?"

"I'm okay." Although she wasn't sure of that at all. "Help me up."

He did so carefully, and soon had her seated in her rocker again. Crandall still sat on the couch, his previously expressionless face now displaying concern.

"I'm sorry," she said automatically.

"You're not the first person I've seen faint. I'm just glad you didn't fall."

"Lovely job you have."

"You had the harder one," he said frankly. "Do you want to see that letter again?"

She nodded, accepting it. The blue CIA logo adorned the top, beneath it the words "Office of the Director."

Now that the shock had passed, she scanned the words below. Not very different from the first letter she'd received from the State Department. A true hero, died in the line of duty serving his country, a sacrifice that would never be forgotten, deep sympathy for her loss… Meaningless.

She stared at it, the words coming in and out of focus. CIA. That was the shocker. It was also an amazing clarifier. She looked at Ryker. "You, too?"

He hesitated, then finally gave her what she needed. "Yes."

"Why the lies?" she asked.

Crandall answered. "State is a cover story. It protects lives, Ms. Hayes. More than you can imagine. Right now, your husband's associates abroad are at risk. That's why we have to ask you to keep this secret. That's why we don't name the stars and why we keep the book so well guarded. A single identity could cause deadly ripples, costing the lives of men, women and children who knew him."

Again she nodded, barely absorbing this. "I need some water." Ryker hurried out and returned swiftly with a glass. She drank half of it in one draft. "How much can I ask?"

"As much as you want. But I'll tell you right now, I know nothing beyond what I told you." Gently, he reclaimed the letter and slipped it into his portfolio. "I'm sorry it took so long to get this to you, but I was assured there were unfolding events. Again, that's the extent of my knowledge." He gave her a half smile. "For obvious reasons, they keep me in the dark."

Another dead end for her. Truth, at last, but a dead end. Except for one thing: Ryker.

Now she knew who he was and how he had lied to her, too.

Rising, she left the room and headed for bed. She was done.

Secrets, Ryker thought as he watched Crandall drive away, were secrets. Omissions. Things not spoken of. To say he worked for State was an outright lie. His cover was blown, the lie revealed, and he wouldn't blame Marisa if she never spoke another word to him.

She had trusted him in so many ways, inviting him into her house and into her bed. He couldn't imagine she would ever trust him again.

He wanted to blow it off. He was used to the price his life exacted, but this was somehow different. He ached for a woman and a fatherless child, and thought that maybe some prices were too high.

Too late now. He'd mucked this up big-time and couldn't see a way back from it. When she'd asked him if he was CIA, too, he'd seen the betrayal in her gaze. Lies. More lies. A big lie from him.

He had told her he wasn't Johnny, but now she knew he was. A liar. A covert operative who couldn't tell the truth about anything. A man who went into danger without telling those who loved them, who might leave them with nothing but an anonymous star and a condolence letter they couldn't keep.

He suspected that, except for his pushing, Marisa might never have received a letter at all. It had happened before. God, he hated it, and the hate was growing deeper by the day.

He knew he'd accomplished important tasks, knew he had helped his country in countless ways, but he had done so while living uncounted lies. Sometimes he wondered if there was a real Ryker inside, or just some amalgam of all the people he'd pretended to be.

For all he knew, deception had become so deeply ingrained that there was nothing real left of him. Except for his feelings about Marisa and her baby. Each time he touched them, he knew they were real. He couldn't afford them, but they existed. They weren't invented. They weren't a part of a job or a ploy.

And he should have known better than to stay here. Once those feelings had reached past his guard, he should have realized the danger in remaining. Not the danger to himself, though this was going to be painful enough, but the danger to her.

Once again he faced the fact that secrecy was different from a lie. He had lied to her. From the instant he had said he worked with Johnny at State, he had sacrificed everything. She would never forgive him.

Oh, she claimed to understand secrecy, and she probably did, but for a long time she had suspected she'd been told lies about John's death. And she had, although he had no idea what the truth was. He was just certain she'd been given a cover story, like everything else.

Then he'd waltzed in, gained her trust and had been proven a liar. Secrecy was no excuse for what he had done to her.

God, he had to get out of this business. He needed to salvage some honesty and decency before he was nothing but a house of someone else's cards.

Or maybe he was already there, about as real as some

figure in a video game, an avatar that called itself Ryker but didn't even really exist.

Not knowing what else to do, he washed off the chicken they'd thawed that morning and started to cook dinner.

He was sure she was going to throw him out. He could at least leave a decent meal for her behind.

The rest of the day passed slowly. Roasting chicken filled the house with delicious aromas. He found the asparagus he'd bought a few days ago and prepared to cook it. He'd make some rice to go with it. After so many years spent mostly abroad, he favored rice over potatoes now.

Pointless exercise. The entire dinner might sit here and spoil.

But then he heard a sound behind him. He turned and saw Marisa. She'd changed into royal blue fleece pants and a top, her belly stretching the fabric. Her eyes had that sunken look again, with big circles beneath them. She'd washed off all the makeup, and he was glad to see it gone. She needed no enhancements.

When she just stood there staring at him, he finally took the plunge, sure that he was going to be crushed on the rocks below. "I'll leave."

"No." She stepped into the room and sat at the table. "No," she said again. "You stay here. I need someone to yell at."

"Fair enough. Milk or something else?"

"Milk. Thank you." Icy. Removed. That hurt more than an eruption.

He brought her the milk, then sat facing her across

the table. He didn't want to loom over her, seem threatening in the least way. Not even unintentionally.

"How's the baby?" he asked presently.

"Better than her mother."

There was nothing he could say to that.

She sipped some milk, then sat staring at the glass, turning it slowly on the table. "You lied to me when you arrived."

"Yes." His chest tightened as if preparing for the blow of a sledgehammer.

"But you didn't lie to me when I asked you earlier."

Where was this going? He couldn't imagine but knew he was going to find out.

"Why?" she asked.

"Why what?"

"You could have lied to me again. Could have told me you were with the State Department, that you had no idea about Johnny. But you didn't, Ryker. That must have broken some kind of operational secrecy."

It had. Most definitely.

"How many other lies did you tell me?"

"None."

"No," she agreed, staring at him now. "No lies. Just a whole lot of omissions and half-truths. How can I ever believe you again?" Her voice had risen, and now she stood, taking her glass of milk and heading for the living room.

He set up a TV table for her in the living room, then brought her a plate full of food, a napkin and utensils. He retreated to eat by himself, but he was only halfway through the foyer when she called him back.

"Ryker. Eat with me."

Well, that amazed him, considering that he figured just looking at him must make her feel sick. Reluctantly, he set up a table for himself, then sat perched on the gooseneck chair with his own meal.

For long minutes she made no move to eat, then with an almost visible shake, she picked up her fork and knife and sliced into the chicken. Only then did he begin to eat himself.

"So, tell me," she said as she ate.

"If I can."

"What's the real reason you don't visit your family and you haven't married?"

"I think you know," he answered.

She surprised him with a glare. "I want to hear it."

The moment of truth. He put down his knife and fork and wiped his mouth with the napkin before he answered. "The truth?"

"As much as you can tell me," she answered bitterly.

"The truth is that I didn't want to leave someone in your position. Because what I did was dangerous and secret, and I refused to be responsible for leaving someone behind to wonder forever. I don't visit my parents because the whole time I'm there I have to skirt the truth and make excuses about why I'm never home, why I've never married, why I haven't given them grandkids. Because the goddamn lies follow me every waking minute of my life!"

The last came out of him with a vehemence that surprised him. He hated the way Marisa shrank back a little as his voice rose.

"Sorry," he mumbled, stabbing at a piece of chicken so hard the fork hit the plate with a clatter. "I wasn't shouting at you."

"Johnny didn't have those qualms."

"Oh, hell." He'd done it again. Awakened a new pain in her. But when he glanced her way, he didn't see anguish. He saw something else he couldn't identify.

Then she abruptly changed the subject. "So you and Johnny are heroes."

"That's debatable. I guess it depends on what side you're on, which parts of the secrets you know, which parts have been hidden from you. John was doing important work. Never doubt it."

"I don't," she said calmly. "Just as I don't doubt that you've done important things. But what the heck? I'll never know, will I? So I guess you have to be your own judge and jury."

That stung. The chicken became tasteless in his mouth. He continued eating only because he needed to.

"Can you tell me just one thing?"

"Ask and I'll see." Even now, he couldn't tell. Even now. God, it sickened him.

"Did Johnny, do you, believe in what you're doing? Or is it all about the thrills?"

The question could have infuriated him, but he didn't let it. "I believed in what I was doing. So did John. It wasn't just for a thrill. Those kinds of thrills nobody needs. The kind of work John and I did…well, you could say we were in the trenches. Not at the embassy balls."

She gave him a half smile that didn't reach her eyes. "No James Bond."

"Not a chance. Pure grunt work and intelligence gathering for the most part. Some infiltration. And now I'm saying too much."

"I can keep secrets, too." She pushed her plate aside. Part of him was sorry about how little she had eaten, but another part was relieved because now he could stop eating, too. It might have been a good dinner, but he couldn't tell. Everything tasted like sawdust.

Which he supposed was another warning. He'd been in worse situations without feeling like this. Situations where he might die at any moment. Nothing had ever reduced him to this abject level of misery. He'd have cheerfully cut out his own beating heart. He'd spent his entire adult life trying to avoid exactly this, but he'd walked into it, anyway. A woman's pain. Her betrayal. Her child. He disgusted himself.

He cleared away the dishes but returned quickly, a niggling fear working on him. She was too calm. At some point… What did he think she was going to do? Kill herself? Not with that baby inside her. He didn't think he'd misjudged her that much.

But he was still worried.

The phone rang. "Want me to get it?"

She shook her head. "It'll be Julie, and I don't want to face the barrage of questions."

"Then, let me." He could do that much for her at least. Julie was indeed full of questions, apparently worried about Marisa, why he was answering instead of her.

"She's feeling under the weather," he answered. A lie or a half-truth? Damned if he knew anymore. "Can I have her call you back tomorrow?"

When he hung up, he knew Julie wasn't satisfied. She'd probably be here soon. Then what?

He sat again, facing Marisa. "I'll give you odds that Julie will be here in the next half hour to check on you."

"I don't want to see anyone."

"I can understand that, but if you think I'm going to be able to successfully hold her off if she shows up, you've got another think coming. She'll be convinced I've murdered you and have your body half hacked up in the bathtub."

Marisa's eyes widened. Then to his absolute amazement, she started to laugh. She laughed so hard that she bent over a little and held her stomach with both arms.

Hysteria? he wondered. She was making him feel so helpless, more helpless than he'd ever felt in his entire life.

But gradually her laughter trailed away, and she wiped tears from her face. "She would," she said. "That's exactly what Julie would think."

"Then let her come. Sorry, but you're going to have to put up with her."

She eyed him. "Then I guess we need our cover story."

The way she said it, she put him on edge. Now she was going to lie to her friends? No way.

"No," he said. "Tell her the whole ugly story. You got news about Johnny today and found out I'm not the guy you thought I was, and you're keeping me around until you're done yelling at me."

"Really?"

"Really. Truth is always better when possible. Don't start covering for me."

Her face softened for the first time in ages it seemed like. "Ryker? Did you make love to me because I wanted it, or because you wanted it?"

That she would even doubt that made him feel as low as a slug. "Oh, I wanted it," he said firmly. "Believe me. The only thing that held me back for so long was that I didn't want to hurt you. I've hurt you, anyway. Story of my life."

"That's not fair," she said quietly. "You just told me

you did without a full life because you didn't want to hurt anybody. I can't say the same about Johnny. He wanted it all. He took it all." She looked down at her stomach and ran her hand over it. "He did leave me something beautiful, though."

"Yes, he did."

She looked up. "And he sent you."

"Marisa…"

She shook her head. "I'm getting past it, Ryker. Why wouldn't I? I've lived with this secrecy for years, and I understand why you couldn't tell me the truth about who you are. I get it. It was just such a shock. CIA never entered my head, but you know what?"

"What?"

"I understand so much now. I'm glad I do. It all finally makes sense."

He wished he could believe this transformation, but he wasn't sure it would last. Maybe she was in a state of shock?

But she sat rocking gently, smiling faintly, her hands protectively over her belly. If today hadn't been such a ride into hell for her, he could have believed that she'd finally found some peace.

And just as he'd predicted, Julie showed up. She stormed past him and surveyed Marisa. "What happened?" she demanded.

"I learned something today," Marisa answered serenely. "Johnny was a true hero. And so is Ryker."

Julie sat slowly. "Really? What did he do?"

"I can't tell you. But it's true." Then Marisa looked at Ryker and smiled. He felt his heart crack wide open. She was one hell of an amazing woman.

Chapter Eleven

Christmas Eve dawned clear and cold. Ryker had returned to Marisa's bed, although he refrained from making love to her. She was content to be held by him, however.

And finally she answered his question. "I do feel peaceful," she said after breakfast. "It's like...just knowing who Johnny worked for, who you work for...it answered questions for me. I get it now, all the secrecy. I get why he could never tell me anything. I suppose, from what you said, that when he was in the Rangers he worked a lot of missions with you."

"That's right," he agreed as he washed the dishes. "His team did a lot of my insertions and extractions. And you didn't hear that from me."

"I didn't hear anything at all." Standing beside him, she shook her head a little and swallowed her prenatal vitamin. "And now I know why nobody would tell me anything. That makes it easier."

He dried his hands and turned around, leaning back against the counter as he drew her into his embrace. He loved looking at her, loved the way the shadows had withdrawn, leaving her face unclouded. Hard to believe that such a parsimonious bit of information could create such a change.

He felt the baby kick against his abdomen and smiled, lifting a hand to stroke her ash-blond hair back from her face. "You're one beautiful, amazing woman."

"Big as a house, too," she retorted.

"An awfully small house," he answered before dropping a kiss on her lips.

"So," she said, shifting her gaze to his chest and resting her hand on him. "When do you have to leave?"

"I don't. Well, I have to go back and resign, but I can do that anytime."

Her head jerked back, and she gaped at him. "Resign? But you said…"

"If you've been listening, I think I've been emitting rumbles of discontent and a desire to change, sort of like a volcano getting ready to erupt. I've made up my mind. I'm done. Cooked. Finished. I'll find something else to do."

"But what?"

He smiled. "I told you, I can take care of myself. Always have. I'll find something."

Ryker was smiling more since Crandall's visit, as if he'd unloaded a burden. Marisa guessed he had. A huge secret had been shed, and she suspected that it had bothered him from the first moment he saw her.

For her own part, she realized now that she trusted him. All the doubts about Ryker had vanished in a searing instant of honesty. Now she knew who he was. Now she knew who Johnny was. Knowing that, it was easier to accept all the things she couldn't know.

Of course, Johnny hadn't died in a street mugging. Her suspicions and doubts had been justified. She'd never know what had really happened, but somehow it was easier to accept knowing that she'd been given a cover story. In some ways, the idea of a cover story to protect lives was a whole lot easier to deal with than the idea that people were wantonly lying to her in order to cover some misdeed.

Now Ryker had decided to resign. She wondered what that would mean for him, for her. Would he stay here in Conard City? Somehow that didn't seem likely to her. He was a man accustomed to traveling the world, to always being in action. How likely was it that he could be content in this backwater?

So she was going to lose him anyway, which saddened her more than she had anticipated. It almost felt like Johnny all over again, but not quite. When Ryker walked away, he was going to live. There'd be no death in this loss, no finality. Maybe they'd be able to keep in touch.

At least she'd know he was out there somewhere in the world, maybe filling all the gaps in his life. Maybe finding a wife, having those kids his parents wanted. She hoped so for him, because more than once she'd gotten the sense that he felt those gaps acutely. He didn't say much about it, but Ryker didn't say a whole lot.

His actions spoke volumes, however. He took care of her, treating her as if she were precious. So, he was a caring man, a rare find. And some of the edge was gone from him, some of the darkness she'd originally sensed. Ryker was waking to a new world.

Just as she had. And looking down at her belly, she felt that she had yet another awakening ahead of her, a joyous one. She and little Jonni were going to build a new, beautiful life. One without secrets. One lived in the bright light of day.

"I'm going out," Ryker said. "I have to pick up a couple of things. Will you be okay for an hour?"

"We'll be just fine," she assured him. Then she said something she never thought she'd say to him. "Hurry back. I'll miss you."

She half expected his face to darken, to react to the implications in those simple words. A man who was about to leave could hardly be happy to realize a woman wanted him back.

But he astonished her. His own face softened, and he came to drop a kiss on her forehead. "I'll hurry," he said huskily. "Want some milk before I go?"

"Ryker!" He pulled a laugh from her. "I'm pregnant, not sick. If I need something I can get it."

"Just don't let me find you on a step ladder."

"On my honor. I think my nesting phase passed."

"Thank God."

She laughed as she heard the door close behind him. After a few minutes she rose and went into her bedroom to look at the crib. Soon a baby would occupy it, turning everything on end. She could hardly wait. She loved picking up the tiny little clothes her friends had given her, still finding it hard to believe they were big enough to fit a baby. Such little bits of clothing, it just didn't seem possible.

But her back had started to ache again, so she returned to the rocker. It wouldn't be long now, she thought, closing her eyes and savoring both her anticipation and impatience. With each passing day, she wanted this baby more, wanted to hold her in her arms, to see the small face, hear the cries. The waiting was becoming intolerable.

Her thoughts wandered to Johnny, and she felt a twinge of familiar guilt. He hadn't even been gone a year. Shouldn't she still be in the pits of grief? But somehow, despite all, she was emerging.

Surely Johnny wouldn't begrudge her that?

But the guilt remained, stinging. Of course she still missed Johnny. Hated the fact that he was dead. Hated that he wouldn't be here to see his child. Sometimes resentment swelled in her, huge and ugly.

But he'd left her here, and she had to keep going. Originally she had done that only for the sake of their child, but now...now she needed to do it for herself, as well.

But she'd always miss Johnny. Always. With him she had forever lost a piece of her heart. But there were pieces left, she realized. A piece for this baby. Pieces for her friend. Maybe even a piece for Ryker.

The ache in her lower back remained. She rocked a little trying to ease it, then, with a gasp, she realized she was sitting in a puddle of water.

Now. Now? Now.

Half-crazed thoughts raced in her head. She picked up the phone Ryker had left beside her, wondering if she should call for an ambulance.

Then she tapped in Ryker's number.

"Hey, you okay?" he answered.

"I think my water just broke."

* * *

Ryker got stopped by a cop for speeding as he raced back to the house from Freitag's. He didn't even wait for the deputy to reach the side of his car.

"Marisa Hayes," he called. "You know her?"

"Yeah."

"Her water just broke."

In an instant he had a police escort with flashing lights and sirens clearing the rest of his way. "God, I love this town," he muttered, his hands gripping the steering wheel until his knuckles were tight.

They pulled up in front of the house, and the cop came inside with him. They found Marisa in her rocker sitting on a towel.

"Ambulance?" the deputy said, ready to key his radio.

Marisa shook her head. "I called the hospital. A ride will do. Ryker?"

"I'll take you."

"Get more towels or I'll ruin your car."

Like he cared about that. But he didn't want to upset her in the least way, so he grabbed a stack of towels and laid them on the passenger seat. The deputy remained to ensure they got safely to the car.

"Any pains?" Ryker asked as they drove toward the hospital on the edge of town.

"Not yet. Just a flood. Ryker…after you leave me there, call Julie. She'll take care of everything, okay?"

"Sure thing." He wished he could take care of everything, but he wasn't family. They probably wouldn't let him anywhere near.

God, he hated it. He had no rights with this woman or her child, and that ate away inside him along with worry.

"Quit looking like this is the end of the world," she said. "It's a baby. Happens millions of times every day."

"Not to you. Not to me." Something perilously close to panic was riding his shoulder.

She laughed quietly. "I feel good. Dang, I feel good! Finally!"

At the emergency room, they helped her into a wheelchair. She gave him her purse. "In case they need any information. And later, I have a small suitcase packed in the closet."

"I'll bring it."

The last thing he saw was her smile and wave as they swept her away.

He stood there feeling helpless, feeling there ought to be something he could do. Hating that he couldn't.

"Be all right, Marisa," he whispered. Then he pulled out his cell phone and called the whirlwind named Julie.

Julie arrived fifteen minutes later, meeting him outside the ER. She walked up briskly, smiling.

"You look awful," she told Ryker. "Relax."

"I can't," he admitted.

"She'll be fine. I'm her coach, so I'll be with her every minute. You get to join the pacing people in the waiting room. Come on up with me and we'll get the news."

That was better than no news at all.

The maternity nurse met them in the waiting room, smiling as if she had the happiest job in the world. "Just in time," she told Julie. "Her first contractions have just started. They warned you first babies take longer, right?"

Julie nodded. "A few of my friends have been down this road. How long do you think?"

The nurse shrugged. "Everyone's different. It might be as long as twenty-four hours."

Oh, God, Ryker thought. He'd had a lot of time lines in his life, but never had twenty-four hours looked longer.

Julie turned to him. "Get some coffee. Go for a run. It's going to be a long haul."

"Just tell someone to keep me posted."

The nurse regarded him. "Who's he?"

"Family," Julie said, surprising him.

"Well, then, I guess we can let you know. But don't hold your breath. First babies take their time."

Locked out, left in a waiting room with an older couple who seemed to be waiting for the same thing, he decided to take Julie's advice. A long run. Then he'd bring back some decent coffee. Maybe he could even slip one to Julie.

As his feet pounded the pavement and icy air stung his face, he wondered how many changes he could make and how fast. Life was suddenly bearing down on him like a freight train.

He needed to get his head straight fast.

Johnna Jayne Hayes was born at 12:07 a.m. on Christmas day. She arrived with one long, loud wail, and then began looking around with bright eyes as if she were delighted to see the world.

A minute later, wrapped in blankets, Johnna was laid in Marisa's arms. Marisa forgot everything else as she stared into that tiny face, into those incredibly piercing dark eyes. *Oh, Johnny, I wish you could have seen her.*

She held her daughter, weariness washing over her in waves, accompanied by a happiness she had scarcely imagined she would find in this moment.

If she hadn't been so tired, she was sure her heart would have burst with joy.

"We have to take the baby for a little while," the nurse said, reaching for Johnna. "The pediatrician needs to check her out. We'll move you to a recovery room. You need some sleep and then you can see her again."

Marisa yielded her daughter only reluctantly. She understood the reasons, but she didn't want to let go. A crazy fear filled her that something bad would happen while the baby was out of her sight.

But even in her weariness she knew that was just a flash from the past. Johnna would receive excellent care; she knew almost everyone who worked here and trusted them. Julie, who had coached her all the way through, sagged against the bed.

"I need some sleep, hon."

"Go home. You were wonderful."

Julie bent over her and dropped a kiss on her forehead. "You get some sleep, too."

"Ryker?"

"Pacing like a caged lion. You want to see him?"

"Please."

"I'll see what I can do."

The fatigue hit Marisa then, and she barely remembered being trundled down the hall and moved to a new bed. Her baby was here, she thought as sleep claimed her.

The world seemed right again for the first time since she got the news.

She awoke later from the deepest of sleeps with no idea of the time. She turned her head a bit and saw Ryker dozing in a chair beside the bed, his eyes closed, his chin propped in his hand.

He must have heard something, because his eyes popped open. "Welcome back," he said, smiling. "By all accounts, you did very well."

"My baby?"

"They won't tell me a lot except that she's perfectly healthy. Oh, and they're going to move you to a regular room soon, and you can have her in a bassinet beside you until they release you."

Instinctively, she reached out a hand, wincing a little as the IV moved. He caught her fingers gently, still smiling, and leaned in to press a kiss on her lips.

"How are you feeling?" he asked softly as he pulled back.

"Exhausted but so very happy."

"Me, too. They let me see her through the nursery window. She's perfect, Marisa, and she looks a lot like both you and John."

A tired laugh escaped her. "How can anyone tell that this soon?"

"It shows." He winked.

She drank him in, thinking she'd never seen him look more rumpled. He looked like he'd gone through a worse time than she had. Maybe so.

A nurse bustled in, throwing Ryker out for a few minutes. "I need to examine her," she explained.

Afterward, the nurse assured her everything was fine, and she'd be moved to a proper room in the next few minutes.

"And my baby?"

"Right behind you," the nurse promised.

Ryker followed her down the hallway to the regular room and then was evicted once again. "Go home, rest, clean up," the woman said. "Marisa needs her rest. Come back in the morning."

Marisa wanted to protest, but Ryker nodded, promised to return first thing in the morning and departed meekly enough.

Marisa watched him walk away and thought that didn't seem fair at all. Mostly, she already missed him.

In the morning, Marisa chose to sit up in a comfortable chair while she nursed Jonni. She was hungry and eager, and Marisa watched her continuously, hardly removing her eyes from the little girl.

Her friends showed up one after another, oohing and aahing and agreeing that Jonni was one of the most beautiful babies they'd ever seen. Marisa accepted their judgment with delight, even though she knew they'd all said the same things about their friends' babies.

But no Ryker. After the girls left, she sat alone with her baby in her arms and felt oddly bereft. He must have left. Certainly he'd been made to feel like an outsider.

But just as she was about to rise and put her baby in the bassinet again, she heard his voice.

"Good morning."

She looked up and saw him standing there smiling, a bouquet in his hand. He added the flowers to the ones the girls had left, then edged closer. "Can I see her? You're looking great."

"I look like a hag." She lifted one hand to try to comb her hair back.

"No, you look beautiful." He stepped closer, and she pulled the receiving blanket back, revealing a small, sleeping face. "Awesome," he said quietly. "Just awesome."

A nurse bustled in—Mary, a woman she knew. The

former sheriff's daughter. "So this is the guy who's been looking after you? Nice to meet you." They shook hands and exchanged names. Then she reached into the cabinet beside the bed and tossed him a folded blue square. "You need to put a gown on before you hold her. We try to send them home healthy." She grinned at Marisa. "It works."

After she buzzed out, Ryker hesitated. He gazed longingly at the baby, but she could tell he didn't want to overstep. And the truth was, letting anyone else hold the child had been impossible so far. Not even her girlfriends.

But something deep within her shifted. "Put on the gown and sit down, Ryker."

He quickly tugged it on so it covered his front and sat in the other chair. Then Marisa rose and carried Jonni to him. Surprisingly, she didn't have to show him how to hold the infant.

Then she returned to her chair and simply watched as a miracle seemed to happen. Ryker's face changed, softening more than she had ever seen it. It was instant love, and she knew it.

She sighed, closing her eyes, and realized she'd just leaped a hurdle. It was okay. Johnny's baby in Ryker's arms. It was as if a circle had been completed.

"Are you tired?" he asked.

She opened her eyes. "A little. But mostly I'm delirious with joy. Come home with us, Ryker. Will you?"

"I never thought of doing anything else."

Three weeks later, life had settled into a comfortable routine. When Jonni woke for her nighttime feedings, Ryker hopped out of bed and brought her to Marisa. Then he'd sit beside them and watch as she nursed. Afterward, he changed the diapers and walked with the baby on his shoulder, gently burping.

"How did you learn how to do all of this?" she finally asked him.

He smiled over Jonni's downy head. "My sister. I was ten when she was born. I have to admit I resented being pushed to take care of her, but I learned a lot even though I tried to avoid it."

"Are you resenting this?" she asked.

"I'm loving it."

The answer warmed her to her toes. During the days he often went out for a while, always returning with some tidbit of food. He took down the Christmas tree without her help while she sat rocking the baby, then spent a couple of hours outside in the cold taking down the lights. Everything was carefully stowed in her basement.

But as settled as he seemed, she worried this was transitory. A man like him couldn't be content with such a bucolic life, she was sure. Like Johnny, before long he'd be running off on his next adventure, never mind what he'd said about resigning from the agency. She didn't really believe that, although she believed he'd meant it when he said it.

Then late one afternoon, Julie popped over unannounced. "I'm babysitting," she announced. "You two need to get out for a while. Take her to dinner, Ryker."

Ryker smiled. "Sounds good to me. Marisa?"

She still hadn't completely regained her shape, and even with the exercises she performed religiously she wondered if she ever would. But she managed to find a pair of slacks with a stretchy waistband and a sweater that covered her worst sins. She liked the way Ryker's eyes devoured her with approval, but she hated knowing this was only temporary. Soon it would be just her and her daughter, and maybe an occasional Skype from some place far away.

Life could be so unfair in some ways, but even as the feeling dampened her mood, she thought of Jonni. Life could also bring amazing joy.

It would be all right, she promised herself. She had a new life to build with her daughter.

The weather was about to turn bad again, and when they arrived at Maude's the place was only half full, a rarity.

She was ravenous these days, and even though her doctor had warned her to be careful, that, yes, she needed more food but not that much, she ordered a steak sandwich and fries. Ryker did the same.

They talked about Jonni for a little while, but then Ryker shifted the conversation.

"I need to go back to DC," he said.

Marisa's heart plummeted. "I thought you must need to," she answered, although she'd been dreading this moment more than she could say...or dared to say. She had no claim on this man. He had come only because Johnny asked him to, and for no other reason. He had a life elsewhere.

"Only long enough to resign," he said firmly.

"Then what?" she asked. "Did you find something?"

"Actually, yes. That cursed ski resort they keep trying to build?"

"The one in the mountains here?" Her heart began to hammer nervously. He was coming back here?

"They're working on it again. But they've decided

they want to lead backcountry hikes during the summer. I've been hired."

Now her mouth started to grow dry. "Really? Will you be happy with that?"

"What I'll be happy with is being with you on weekends all summer, and then every day in the winter."

She felt her jaw drop a little. "Ryker?"

He looked down at his plate. "You know, there can't be any place less romantic than this. There's a storm brewing outside and a baby and Julie waiting at home. So, please, excuse me if the atmosphere is lacking, but what I'm trying to say is, if you'll have me, I love you and want to marry you."

She couldn't find her voice. Her heart had climbed into her throat, where it nearly suffocated her. She hardly dared believe what she was hearing.

His expression turned rueful. "Guess this doesn't make you happy."

She fought for a breath, knowing it was now or never. This man would vanish as soon as he took her home if she let him believe that.

"No," she burst out.

His face sagged a little. "Sorry if I made you uncomfortable."

"Ryker, no. That's not...not what I meant." She dragged in another lungful of air. "God, I'd been so afraid that you'd leave me. I love you!"

Watching his expression change was one of the most beautiful things she'd ever seen. A smile was born on that harsh face, and every line lifted.

"To hell with it," he said.

The next thing she knew he'd slipped out of the booth

and was kneeling beside her, heedless of gawkers or the sudden complete silence in the diner.

"Marisa Hayes, will you, please, marry me?"

"Yes," she breathed. Then she threw her arms around his neck. "Yes, yes, yes!"

She hardly heard the applause from those around them. She felt nothing except a heart full to bursting with a dream come true. He loved her. He was going to stay.

All she had ever wanted had just swept into her life and carried her away to the joy she had never thought she would feel again.

Thank you, Johnny, she thought. He'd given her a child, and now he'd sent her love. A legacy and a gift.

The tears that rolled down her face now were purely happy, and Ryker's arms around her were a promise for a brighter future.

Epilogue

They were married on Valentine's Day. Julie and her friends had taken over completely, and Marisa, wearing a simple white gown, walked down the aisle in Good Shepherd Church, surrounded by what seemed like half the people in town. Ryker's father escorted her, to stand in for her own long-gone father.

Ryker awaited her along with the pastor. Julie wore a red bridesmaid dress and held a tiny Jonni, who was also swaddled in red. Beside Ryker, Hank stood as groomsman.

Snow fell outside the tall windows, but it fell gently, purifying the world. Inside, no shadows reached any corner. As Marisa passed the front row, Ryker's mother suddenly stood and leaned over to kiss her cheek.

"Welcome to the family," the woman said warmly.

Marisa smiled at her, her heart so filled with joy she was certain it must encompass the whole world.

I love you, Johnny, she thought. *I will always miss you. Thank you for Ryker.*

She could almost feel him on her other side, as if he too walked her down the aisle. Then she reached Ryker, and every other thought fled as magic touched her once again.

Full circle. Life and love had returned.

* * * * *

Look for the next book in
New York Times *bestselling author Rachel Lee's*
CONARD COUNTY:
THE NEXT GENERATION *miniseries,*
coming in 2017 from Harlequin Special Edition.

And don't miss out on previous
CONARD COUNTY: THE NEXT GENERATION
books from Special Edition:

A COWBOY FOR CHRISTMAS
THE LAWMAN LASSOES A FAMILY
A CONARD COUNTY BABY

SPECIAL EDITION

Available August 23, 2016

#2497 A MAVERICK AND A HALF
Montana Mavericks: The Baby Bonanza • by Marie Ferrarella
Anderson Dalton is suddenly a daddy—to a ten-year-old! Romance is the last thing on his mind, but love finds him in the form of Marina Laramie, a schoolteacher with a bouncing baby of her own. Marina offers a marriage of convenience, just for the kids' sake, of course. But when long-kept secrets come out, will their fake marriage have a chance to become the real deal?

#2498 A CAMDEN'S BABY SECRET
The Camdens of Colorado • by Victoria Pade
Widowed Livi Camden had only ever kissed her late husband and is sure he was her only chance at love and happiness. At least until one wild night on a Hawaiian business trip leaves her pregnant with former bad boy Callan Tierney's baby. Will career-minded Callan and still-grieving Livi be able to give their new family a chance?

#2499 HER TEXAS RESCUE DOCTOR
Texas Rescue • by Caro Carson
Grace Jackson has been the unassuming, overworked personal assistant to a Hollywood movie star all her life—after all, the movie star is her big sister. To save her sister's career from bad publicity, Grace turns a quiet geek of an emergency room doctor, Alex Gregory, into the perfect escort for a celebrity-studded charity ball. But has she created the perfect man for her sister...or for herself?

#2500 A WORD WITH THE BACHELOR
The Bachelors of Blackwater Lake • by Teresa Southwick
Erin Riley has a new gig as a book coach with bestselling author Jack Garner. He may be a monosyllabic grump, but she's never been this drawn to a client. Jack is beginning to believe he is a one-hit wonder and doesn't want to be pulled into her sunny disposition. These two might have opposite personalities, but maybe that's what will help them heal their equally battered hearts.

#2501 MEET ME AT THE CHAPEL
The Brands of Montana • by Joanna Sims
Rancher Brock McCallister hasn't found much to laugh about recently, but when eternal optimist Casey Brand moves into the apartment above the barn, she brings much-needed light into his autistic daughter's life...and his own. When tragedy strikes, he must convince Casey that the three of them can be the family she's always wanted and the second chance at love he deserves.

#2502 THE COWGIRL'S FOREVER FAMILY
The Cedar River Cowboys • by Helen Lacey
The last thing Brooke Laughton expected to see when she opened her door was sexy lawyer Tyler Madden with a baby in his arms. Turns out, she has a niece! While they wait for her brother to return and claim the baby, Brooke and Tyler give in to a deep attraction, but old fears threaten to keep them apart.

YOU CAN FIND MORE INFORMATION ON UPCOMING HARLEQUIN® TITLES, FREE EXCERPTS AND MORE AT WWW.HARLEQUIN.COM.

SPECIAL EXCERPT FROM

H HARLEQUIN®

SPECIAL EDITION

A makeover, a doctor, a movie star.
It should be the beginning of a red-carpet romance,
but Dr. Alex Gregory is more interested in the
unassuming assistant, Grace Jackson,
who just happens to be the movie star's sister.

Read on for a sneak preview of
HER TEXAS RESCUE DOCTOR,
the new book in Caro Carson's
***TEXAS RESCUE** miniseries.*

Alex didn't wait for a request to stand next to Grace. He walked up to her, tuning out the cluster of people who'd invaded his house. "You look very, very beautiful."

"Thank you."

Princess Picasso gave an order. "You two should dance. I need to see if I'll be able to move in it. What kind of music are they going to be playing, anyway?"

Grace didn't look away, so neither did he, but she answered her sister. "Some country-and-western bands. Pretty big names. We have a dance lesson scheduled later today."

"I know how to waltz and two-step." Alex stepped closer and picked up her hand. "Do you?"

"I waltz." They assumed the traditional position of a man and a woman in a ballroom dance, and Alex took the first step.

Grace's voice was as lovely as everything else about her. She counted to three over and over in a little nonsense melody, smiling at him, his beautiful golden girl, silver in his arms, glowing with happiness.

He realized he was smiling back.

So this is happiness. He recognized it, although it had been a very long time since he'd felt it. It was not equilibrium. There was no balance. He was absolutely at the far end of a scale, a feeling of pure pleasure unadulterated by pain—yet.

There was always pain. He knew that, but at this moment, he couldn't imagine ever feeling pain again, not with Grace in his arms.

"One, two, three. One, two, three."

"You look wonderful," the stylist said, clapping. "Sophia, what do you think?"

He and Grace had to stop, or risk looking like fools. She gave his hand a friendly squeeze as she stepped out of his arms. A *friendly* squeeze. Friends. There was pain in being friends with someone he desired so keenly.

Don't miss
HER TEXAS RESCUE DOCTOR by Caro Carson,
available September 2016 wherever
Harlequin® Special Edition books and ebooks are sold.

www.Harlequin.com

THE WORLD IS BETTER WITH

Romance

Harlequin has everything from contemporary, passionate and heartwarming to suspenseful and inspirational stories.

Whatever your mood, we have a romance just for you!

Connect with us to find your next great read, special offers and more.